I0692320

THE COLUMBUS DAY CONSPIRACY
BY
GIBRAN TARIQ
&
GREGORY STANTIN JONES

THE COLUMBUS DAY CONSPIRACY

©2017 by Gibran Tariq & Gregory Stantin Jones

ACKNOWLEDGEMENTS
Gibran Tariq

Above all else, all praise is due to Allah, the Creator of the heavens, the earth, and all between.

I cannot fathom dedicating this other to anyone other than the members of my family: my sisters: Charlotte, Lorraine, Valerie, Jacqueline, Carolyn Denise, Gwendolyn, Angela, and Paula; my brothers, Buddy Cool, Brotha Dave, Butch, and John; my daughters, Latonya, Adrienne, Shameka, and Joy; my grandchildren, and all my wonderful nieces and nephews.

Others I must acknowledge include Mrs. Joan Boudreaux, the very first person to believe in me and who wouldn't permit me to give up. Without her guidance, I would have given up.

I must also thank Sista Laylah and Sista Angela Morrow, both of whom have been vital in my survival as a writer.

At every step I've taken during the course of my life, I have enjoyed the luxury of good company, and I feel compelled to salute my comrades and hustling partners with whom I spent many years in the trenches with: RL Morrow, James "Flint" Wells, Napoleon "Napo" Melton, Jafar (Odell Ware), DC Mobley, Malik (Keith Ross), O'Neal "Hard-Times" McGill, Jihad Omar Hasan, Ahmad (Marty Rorie), Hassan (Lenny White), Jamal (Johnell Porter), Abdullah (Leon Funderburke), Turk Maxwell, Larry Manns, James, "JB" Brown, Chris Bailey, Curt Riley, Ronald Brown, Ronald Dixon. Last but not least, I salute two of my hustling mentors, Billy Dykes and Billy Brown.

I submit that I am very pleased to have had the opportunity to work with Gregory "Bo" Jones whom I met while in the fed joint in Atlanta. Had it not been for the five years of research he did, this work could never have materialized. The brother is a great writer and you will be hearing a lot from him in the future. This brotha is still in the federal prison in Atlanta where he has been for over 25 years. I ask that you keep him in your prayers. Keep your head up, Bo. I got your back!

Salaam to the many good, good brothas I have "Deened" with in the joint: Imam Ali Hasan, Wali Rashid, Idris Saifullah, Supreme Justice Shabazz, Uthman, Dawud Shabazz(RIP), Yusef(Gregory Webb) Mullah X, Mumin, Aziz, Fenyang Richardson, Mujahid Herbie, and all the other brothers from the Ummah at Eastern Correctional, and The Walls!

And speaking of friends, I must thank two of the best: Herbie Lee McKinney (Manuel), and his cousin, Herbie Lee McKinney who looked out for my sisters when they were in High School! Thanks

ACKNOWLEDGEMENTS
Gregory Stantin Jones

Thanks are given to the Almighty Creator God, then my kids, Ungenita, Arleshia, and Kent. I thank them for all the pleasure they have brought me in my life, and for putting up with their father not being home. I especially thank my mother, Ozella Jones, and my aunts, Ann Jones, and Gloria Lee Boswell, who, from day one, literally stood by me and supported me through the good and the bad times. I also give acknowledgments to other members of my family: my grand-kid, Shawnquavius, Tytiana, JaCorey, Imani, DeShawn, Linniah, Javanni; my sister, Ungenita Prevost; my brother, Reginald; my aunts, Shirley, Mable, Bernice, Gaynell, and Mozell; my uncles, Willie, James, Pinkin, John, June-Bug, Catfish, and Johnny; my cousins, Gary, Joyce, Gabriell, Gary Jr,, Gayla, Kim, Jerald, Tan Tan, Tanisha, Quincy, Terrell, La Nikka, Sharmaine, Tieyoner, Chanell, Jarnard, Shanta, Marcus, and Felical.

In loving memory, a special acknowledgment goes out to my late wife, Linda D. Jones; my grandmother, Mrs. Princella Boswell; my grandfather, Governor Sam Jones, and also Mrs. Geraldine Beech. I thank you all for all your love. I pray that God will keep you all in spiritual peace.

I would like to thank the following people for their contributions, encouragements and inspiration: Antoine Wells, Calvin Thomas, Tracey E. Squire, Robert "Batman" Edwards, Robert "Big Shag" Lane, Jermaine Hopkins, Brenda McKinney, Tyrone Walker, Pierre "N.O.L.A." Parsee, Phillip Wyatt, Keith Hill, Chad "N.O." Payne, Jermaine Tarkin, Frederick Miles, L, Boswell, Lloyd Williams, Jerry, Berry, Dirt, Allan Poulnott, Ike Perry, Matthew Brown, Terry. C. Jenkins, Kathy Arnold, Ms. Marianita Jenkins, Ms. Sakeenah Hasan, Emerson Ledwell-Bey, Ms. Rebecca Bowman, Othis Hasty, Donald Davenport, Ms. Diedra Randolph, Theodous Williams, Frank Sharpe, MB-Edward, Antonio Sadler, Terry Savage-El, Bobby Gates, Joel Williams, Emmanuel Terrell, Robert Moss Jr., Rico Carter, Clarence Jones, Johnnie Reed, and many others. Thanks again.

Lawrence Martin, you are acknowledged for all the hours you spent developing the (original) front cover. Thank you for a beautiful and excellent piece of art work.

This book is greatly due to the conversation held over the years with my good friend, Gibran Tariq. So much is due to him. I'm very, very proud to have worked with Mr. Tariq on this book which we began writing September 1st, 2001. I really enjoyed our work in shaping and expressing the knowledge shared on these pages, and I pray this book will not be the ending but the beginning on many more. Your friendship is deeply appreciated and again I would like to thank God for having our paths cross to make this possible.
Thank You All
B.S. Jones

ONE

NOVEMBER 1942

It was one thing to be cold, but quite another to be freezing. Not long ago, Paul Madsen had been warm and safe and at home. Now, he was in New York where his mind raced to find a way to rouse up some inner warmth. With nearly everything else having failed, he imagined himself back home in England, and for a while the charade worked. He actually forgot about how cold and how miserable he actually felt, but within a few seconds, a harsh wind soured him on the game he was playing.

Yet the blistering cold was not the only difficulty Madsen faced. He was dying, literally falling apart internally at what one doctor had said was an unimaginably quick pace, and as recently as two weeks ago, another doctor had whispered that what he was, in essence, was a dead man walking. So maybe the cold, bitter wind was a bargain, he thought. To feel it meant he was still alive, but the all-consuming question was: *how much longer?!*

Paul Madsen tucked his thin neck down deeper into the collar of his expensive overcoat, snuggling the downy shawl tighter around his throat. He pushed on. He had seen how nimble death could be so he fought the wind, seeking to expand his lead on the Grim Reaper. Somehow, he had to exploit the promise of the one good deed he hoped would grab God's attention, and cinch for him a sumptuous grant of divine mercy. Boy, did he need it.

He walked even faster.

With so many different directions to go in, he lost his focus momentarily, and when the howling North wind warned him that the temperature could fall even more dangerously low, he found the idea quite unattractive. He gazed at the sky, finding even less beauty in the appeal of the approaching darkness. Night, with its terrifying blackness, was swiftly approaching like a winged messenger of impending doom.

He walked even faster.

Desperation clutched at his inner resolve, and since there was practically nothing left of his weakened lungs, when the souped-up cough surged up from the depths of his bowels, he instinctively sensed that the end was near. At its peak, the wracking cough would normally only paralyze him until his strength matured enough to stabilize him, but this time, he was crippled internally, and knocked to his knees. Liquid, green snot dripped from his dilated nostrils at high speeds while the phlegm that stagnated in his tightly constricted chest exploded into his throat becoming vomit so translucent, it sprayed from his gagging mouth like polluted water.

Regaining his feet, he rocked to and fro in his exquisitely hand-crafted shoes, sure that death was muscling in on his turf.

Alone, he stood in the grim blackness that the night had conjured up, steering his wobbly legs across a flat street that rolled down a steep hill next to a diner.

"Hey, man," he shouted at a passerby, "please sir, tell me where do the niggers live?"

When Madsen burst into another spasm of god-awful coughing, the man frowned in disgust, and quickly walked away. He wanted to have nothing to do with anyone that wretchedly ill, especially at a time when no one had money for medicine.

Left with no choice, Madsen pulled himself together, and after a brief but valiant struggle, managed to achieve a tiny measure of respectability. He boldly flung himself into the welcoming warmth of the cavernous restaurant, but was immediately seized with the panic that the hacking cough would return, and that the patrons, sensing he had tuberculosis, would unmercifully pitch him out into the snow to die. He couldn't risk that. He couldn't imperil the mission that had brought him so far from home because what real value was there in dying incomplete? He would do what he had come to do, and driven by this euphoria, aggressively strolled across to the counter at a robust clip.

By the time he reached the counter, he had collected a big piece of his inner resolve, and though he realized his request would raise eyebrows, it wasn't that ridiculously outrageous.

"Excuse me, kind sir," Madsen said warmly, "but I can't seem to find any niggers, and I'm in dire need of one. Could you tell me where they live?"

"Ah," the diner's owner nodded knowingly. "I see."

Reading the man's thoughts, Madsen quickly blurted. "Oh no, not for that." He blushed. "I sorry if I misled you. I'm not a pervert. It's just that---."

"It's none of my business," the owner snapped, "but just the same, we don't cater to them 'round here."

"Still, you must---?"

The owner stared at Madsen coldly. "I don't know where you're from, but in this country, we're not obsessed with those people. You a foreign correspondent of some sort?"

Madsen shook his head. The incessant demand to cough was tumbling round and about in his lungs, and he predicted that it wouldn't be long before he was swallowed up in an avalanche of fitful retching. His bowels were already starting to swell with noxious gases. "Please," he begged.

Aroused by Madsen's pleading, the owner spoke cheaply. "If you're not a fag or a commie news reporter, what would you do in coon-town?"

"Knock on any door...." Madsen stopped. He would burst the man's bubble. He would leave. "I am sorry. I have come to the wrong place." He hobbled towards the front door, the need to cough propped up by the dragging down of all the moisture in his mouth. "I bid you farewell."

"Wait."

Madsen stopped, but kept his back to the man. "Are you talking to me?"

"Go into the kitchen, through that door. Bernie is back there."

Madsen turned slowly. *"Bernie?"*

"Yeah, Bernie," the owner rasped, "a real-live nigger."

<<<<<
SOULFIRE BOOKS
<<<<<

Madsen hurriedly pushed through the swinging doors, roughly dispelling the air bagged in his throbbing chest. He was doubled over by the force of the impact, and now adding to his woes was a ragged fever.

Straightening himself up, Madsen spied an elegant-looking black man in a chef's hat and apron. The man instantly took a step backwards. Madsen grinned, knowing that the aura of doom that surrounded him could not have been inviting. "You may not believe it, Bernie, but today is the luckiest day of your life." Then he collapsed to the floor.

Moments later when he regained consciousness, it came as no surprise to Madsen when he found the black man was nursing him, had loosened his shirt, and was wiping his brow with a cold, damp cloth.

"Thanks," Madsen offered weakly. He reached into his coat pocket. "It seems as if you have already earned this." He shoved an envelope into Bernie's hand. "Here, take this," he commanded softly, "there isn't much time."

"Who are you?" Bernie asked suspiciously. He glanced at the envelope with even greater concern. "And, what is this?"

Summoning the last of his well-known iron will, Madsen tried to stand, but found it difficult, so he insisted that Bernie help him to his feet. "Is there anywhere we can have a bit of privacy?"

"This way." Bernie escorted Madsen to a table.

Once seated, Madsen knew he had to talk fast. There wasn't much time left. He coughed, glad it was only a mid-tempo roar, and composing himself, he pointed to the envelope. "War bonds. Also some stock certificates." He stared at the black man. "They're yours."

"*Why?*"

Madsen ignored the question. "As bearer of these bonds and certificates, whenever you're ready to start living like a king, all you have to do is to redeem them. That's all it takes. Everything is endorsed--."

"*Why?*"

When Madsen stopped coughing, he spoke wearily. "You're rich, Bernie. You're the richest black man the world has ever seen." When Bernie fell back, clutching his chest, Madsen grinned triumphantly. "You do understand, then?"

"I know about war bonds," Bernie confessed.

"There's nothing you really need to know. I have taken care of everything. You're filthy rich, Bernie, just like I was." Madsen winced. "Easy come, easy go."

A tear rolled from the black man's eyes. "May the Lord---"

"Yeah, yeah," Madsen grumbled, "my sentiments exactly, but I've been a very evil, mean person." He shrugged casually. "Trouble is, I've enjoyed the dickens out of being me, the infamous Paul "Mad-Dog" Madsen." For a brief while, he felt absolutely giddy, but soon he was coughing and wheezing again. Turning increasingly paternal, he stuffed his hand into another pocket of his coat. "The stocks and bonds were for you. Do you have any children?"

Bernie nodded.

"Well, this is for your children's children's children." Madsen handed Bernie a simple, unadorned jewelry box.

"I-I don't understand."

"And you probably never will, but listen carefully. What's inside this box is highly valuable, and to be quite honest, people will kill to get their hands on those documents."

Bernie gulped. *"Documents!?"*

"Don't fear. As long as you keep them in your family, passing the box along from generation to generation, all will be well." Madsen gripped Bernie's arm tightly. "No one outside of your family must ever know about this box, understand?"

Bernie nodded.

"Good, because it is very, very important that you understand this." Madsen lowered his voice. "To say anything to anyone about the contents of this box would..." He paused. "Simply put, it would bring about the total and immediate destruction of your entire family."

"By who?!"

"Your government," Madsen croaked. "Your president." Madsen released his grip. "You have been warned. I can do nothing more."

"Th-these document," Bernie stammered fearfully, "what are they?"

"Enough to destroy this country." Madsen felt stronger. "There is a duplicate of what you have in that box stashed away in a private Swiss bank account, but international bankers and an assortments of other rogues may eventually sniff it out."

"Wh-what happens then?" Bernie timidly quizzed.

Madsen sighed. "If that happens, then everything will go to your descendants."

"Then what?"

"Then what?" Madsen laughed merrily. "They will own the whole damn country, that's what!"

TWO

NOVEMBER 2002

There was no other way to describe it. Tolliver Merchant felt as if he was glowing. It had started shortly after he had left the Grantsmith Plaza, but still it was hard for him to believe how easily he had gotten away with it. He had won, and damn what a victory it had been.

What was most peculiar about the whole meeting was why Gulliver, his twin brother, hadn't put up more of a fight. How odd, especially since everyone damned well knew the bastard wanted to run Quicksilver Properties, the real estate company their father, Gideon, had founded. And at this moment, this puzzled him. The New York-based corporation carried far more than mere sentimental value as neither brother was fiercely loyal to any particular sentiment. However, what Quicksilver did represent, though, was a bonafide business whose stock had, just last week, hit an all-time dollar high which, on average, had topped any other real estate stock ever traded publicly.

"The son-of-a-bitch took a dive," Tolliver mumbled to himself, but loud enough so that Jason Caldech could make out what he had said. "Gully let me screw him. Why?"

Caldech made a face, then tapped himself lightly upon his right temple. "Maybe he's smarter than you." He shrugged his shoulders absently. "Maybe he saw the ghost of your father when he was sitting there, and decided that any fucking thing was better than what--."

"Dad was good at what he did, dammit, and you, of all people, should understand that."

Caldech sighed. "Great men know when to quit, Tully. Your father didn't, and that's why the company ate him alive. Ate him like he was some sort of human delicacy, and then spit him out." He tapped himself upon his temple once more. "Gully remembers what he saw, and he's smart enough not to want ulcers and a shithouse full of other psychosomatic ailments."

"Smart, huh," Tolliver grunted. "A few months ago, the bastard would have auctioned off his first-born for the chance to fill dad's shoes. I don't get it. First you, then him"

Caldech leaned forward in his chair. "Listen, Tully, to be honest with you, I can't begin to explain why your brother didn't challenge you for the presidency of the empire, but the reason I made way for you is because I'm too old for this shit." He chuckled mirthlessly. "Plus, I like my money without a whole helluva lot of misery chasing it."

"Drink?"

"My usual please."

Tolliver, tall, blond, and ambitious, vacantly studied his father's best friend. Even at sixty-eight, Jason Caldech still reminded him of Doctor Spock, the Vulcan on Star-Trek, but now, it wasn't so much the physical resemblance. It was how precise and logical he was. Nothing escaped his attention, and he had the uncanny ability to always put just the right spin on everything that was going on around him. Other than this, he was very ordinary.

Tolliver, a forty year old, self-proclaimed business whiz, made fresh drinks. "Could you believe that suit Gully had on?"

"Hmmph," Caldech snorted, "probably cost more than yours. By the way, you look like a damn mortician. Gully's get-up had, what do the young kids' call it. Yeah, attitude. That's it. Gully's suit had guts."

"Knock it off, Jay. You know what I'm getting at."

"I do?"

"Hell yeah. No businessman of sound mind comes to the biggest corporate fight of his life without a power suit on. That suit Gully had on, given the nature of the meeting was the equivalent of any great boxer stepping into the ring to fight for the championship of the world wearing a pair of pink trunks."

Caldech rubbed his chin thoughtfully. "I'll let you be the judge of that. Meanwhile, I'll protect your ass. You protect our assets."

"So you do think that Gully's play out there this morning is something that bears suspicion?"

Caldech, for once, appeared visibly shaken. "Okay, okay," he gestured with his hands, "so it did throw me for a loop because he should have come out swinging for all he was worth."

"The bastard is going for something, Jay. I can feel it. What does he want?"

"If he had any sense, the whole shebang, that's what."

"But that's an impossible dream if there ever was one." Tolliver released the knot from his tie. "Isn't it?"

Caldech thought that over. "I admit, we're strong, but a good rule of thumb to keep in mind is that anything one jackass can build, another jackass can steal."

"But with new revenue opportunities throughout all our units, where is it conceivable that he'll---"

"Hold on to your damn horses, will you. We can't put a saddle on a horse until we first rope it, so if we have a problem, we must first identify it."

"Dammit, Jay, my brother is the problem."

"Well, I'll tell you this. As top-dog, you had better develop a knack for fixing problems, or else I will unveil a scheme to get your ass kicked out so quickly that it will make your head swim."

Beyond huffing and puffing, Tolliver displayed nothing more visible of how much that remark had stung him. He merely stared at the bottom of his glass, choosing to remain silent, but the ensuing gloom felt like a near-death experience. "Gully is no match for me, whatever his bullshit," he finally blurted. "I just grew brass balls."

<<<<<
SOULFIRE BOOKS
<<<<<<

William "Bill" Dudley, a short, red-headed man-about-town, was semi-retired, and had recently fled New York for the more idyllic vista of Jackson Township, but the gated community where he lived in New Jersey unnerved Gulliver. Despite the eighteen hole golf course, the two pools, and the luxury clubhouse, everything seemed lifeless and antiseptic without the rattle and hum of children. Kids were banned from living in Greenbriar Westlake.

Siting in the den, Gulliver gazed out of the window at the neat suburban tracts across the street, and with a practiced eye for detail, could easily discern how affluent the community was. Everyone was loaded.

"And I bet you had me pegged as the typical nuts-and-bolts Florida type," Dudley remarked after checking on the steaming kettle of ginseng tea. "Don't let the gray hairs fool you because everyone around here is in top-notch shape. Age-restricted refers only to the housing concept, not the shenanigans." He winked slyly. "I'm having the time of my life."

"That's all well and good," Gulliver retorted rudely, "but my drive out here was not meant to be social."

"I guess you're wondering---"

"Damn right, Bill. What the hell you think? You couldn't have gotten me out here any quicker if you had taken my family hostage. And this had better be good because that frantic phone call of yours caused me to piss away my chances of running QuickSilver. It was very likely, I could have won hands down in a vote against Tully. With the exception of Jay, I had most of the major players in my pocket, and now I've got some explaining to do."

"Forget it. Tell the greedy bastards to kiss your ass." Dudley waved his hands expansively. "Don't feel like you own them shit because what's getting ready to come down is no Wizard of Oz bullshit." Dudley made a screwed-up face. "In the end, before this little fiasco runs its course, a lot of executives are going to end up with slashed wrists."

Gulliver pushed forward in his chair. "Wh-what's coming down the line, Bill? Are you an insider?"

"No dice, Gully. We're all outsiders on this one. Sorry. What's worse is that I don't know how much of a chance there may be to keep the damages sustainable."

"You're scaring me, dammit. If Quicksilver is prey---."

"Gully, listen, the whole economy is prey, and if that scares you, then I don't know how you're going to take this because I believe in calling a spade a spade."

Gulliver swallowed the air trapped in his chest. "I have always valued and trusted your opinion, and I've settled many a score based on your advice." He gulped. "If you say it's bad, then I believe you."

Dudley sighed in relief. "Day before yesterday, I entered into discussion with a dearly trusted friend. For decades, he has been a Swiss banker and knows where most of the world's financial dirt is hidden, and who's hiding it, but even he claims he has never seen anything like this."

"This?"

"Certain documents."

"Documents. Of what nature?"

Dudley sighed. "Purposely, he left me without a lot of information, but I do understand the documents to be highly complex instruments used to ease the sting of a crushing debt."

"Please, Bill, dispense with all the riddles. Who owned what to whom, and why was it paid in such a peculiar fashion? That does seem to be what you implying, isn't it? That this huge debt was paid--."

"The debt was never paid."

"But you just said that the documents..." Gulliver struggled for words. "If the debt wasn't paid, just what in the world were the documents used for?"

"Collateral," Dudley hissed. "The documents, numbered and hidden in a Swiss bank account, were surety for a debt incurred---"

"Fix me a drink," Gulliver interrupted dismissively, "and tell me about your bailout plan.'

Dudley stared through Gulliver. "You're not listening, Gully. This is no scheme, no scam, no smokescreen. This is a real American nightmare."

"Oh shit," Gulliver groaned, slapping the desk angrily. "The market is getting ready to take a dive on account of these documents, right?"

"Worse, Gully. Much worse. The whole country is getting ready to nosedive into a big pile of shit. Everything will change and no one will be exempt. Nothing will ever be the same again. *Ever.*"

Shaking his head slowly from side to side, Gulliver groaned some more. "Just what in God's name did your friend tell you?"

When Dudley cleared his throat, it sounded digitally amplified like a special effect in a sci/fi movie. "Do you have any idea what the second Monday in October is?"

Gulliver shrugged in annoyance. "Someone's birthday?"

"Columbus Day."

"For Christ's sake, Bill, what does Columbus Day have to do with any of this? Jesus," Gulliver rasped. "Just tell me what your Swiss banker friend said. Anyway, I thought this was about some high-velocity documents."

"It is. At any rate on Columbus Day, these documents will be released per the agreement of the depositors of the document."

"Were you, by chance, eligible for any info concerning the identity of these so-called depositors?"

Dudley nodded. "They are all dead and gone, and have been for quite some time."

"What?"

"Hear me out," Dudley cautioned. "The deceased were no less than the premier money lenders of their day. All were foreign bankers, the cream of the crop, and true to type, this was no bunch of angels."

"Let him who is without sin, cast the first stone."

Dudley smiled, unperturbed by the insinuation. "Gully, this is the end of the world as we know it. This time the sky really is falling."

[Circa 1933. That was when this incident had started. There was evidence that Paul "Mad-Dog" Madsen was as shrewd a banker as could possibly exist at that time in London, and as if that wasn't enough, he was also the principal strategist behind a secret cartel of foreign investors who fretted over the declining value of their investments in America. Fearing that the American economy was on the verge of collapse, he devised a plan to reign in Uncle Sam's debt. Unfortunately, though, America had just witnessed the crash of '29, and had absorbed all of its overseas credit, and odds were very good that the country would not survive without the buy-out leverage of foreign investors. Added to these woes was the fact that gross domestic production in the States had fallen to new, absolute lows.

Stunned bankers from England and France sharply cut back on their lending, and by the time America had declared bankruptcy the following year, money from all outside sources had dried up totally].

"You can bet your sweet ass that Mad-Dog was afraid to take a hit, but he knew that he had to either shit or get off the pot." Dudley sipped his steaming tea. "I believe he felt that to do nothing would be like throwing the baby out with the bath water. He felt, more than likely, that if he could stop the slippage by ten percent, he could manage to prevent any more major losses."

"So Madsen took it upon himself to become Mr. Crunch-Time."

"Hell, from what I could pull up on the old geezer, it was him or no one else. The man was mythical; part Scrooge, part Alan Greenspan, part Midas."

Gulliver grinned. "Partly insane. Who would risk loaning money to a country with no gold or silver as security?"

"Mad-Dog Madsen. Plus, who needed gold or silver when you have--."

"The documents," Gulliver mimicked,

"Correct."

Gulliver shook his head. "Documents or not, to risk money like that was not sane, and it puzzles me to see where any documents that lacked the ability to shit gold bricks could be worth spilling ink on." He sighed. "What are the documents and what is their shelf life?"

"What do you think birth certificates are all about, and I urge you to forget the obvious shit that automatically pops to mind because you would be wrong by a mile."

Gulliver sat up in his chair as if he had been shocked, his face darkened, then turned cloudy as he fumbled for words. "D-don't tell that our birth certificates...." Realizing instantly what had come about, he attempted to rekindle the fire in his voice, but he could not quite manage it. "You mean…"

Dudley nodded. "Welcome to the club, Gully. The birth certificates of American citizens are the documents. The country put us all up as collateral for the debt. Smart, huh? It would have been harder to find anything else more suited to satisfy a debt than people. Shrewd bastard, that Madsen,"

Gulliver couldn't argue the wisdom of that. Pundits had always applauded the fact that the people were a country's most valued commodity, but it had taken Paul Madsen to find the price tag. And yes, it was as smart as hell. "Bet that really put a notch on that joker's belt."

"And made the rest of us slaves."

"*Slaves?!*"

"Wise up, Gully, for Pete's sake. We're property. Some bastard owns us."

"Madsen….."

"Not Madsen. Plus, he is dead and gone. In any event, advancing age must have softened Mad-Dog up because shortly before he died, he had one last deal to pull off. He couldn't take his fortune with him so he successfully bought out all the other horsemen of this apocalypse, and with all the documents under his control, he established a Swiss bank account."

"How damn humanitarian is that?" Gulliver rasped. "Sounds like business as usual for a robber baron."

Dudley took a deep breath. "Here's the bottom line, Gully, and it's not pretty. I guess you can't begrudge a sinner at death's doorsteps from trying to court the favor of the Lord, and to win a pardon from hell by doing a tremendous work of goodwill."

Gulliver held up his hand to stop Dudley. "I'm not interested in his business with God. How does this bullshit affect me so, for the last time, what did Madsen do?"

"It's virtually unimaginable, but he established a system where the documents would be parceled out this Columbus Day---"

"Good grief, this can't get any more ludicrous, can it?"

Dudley ignored the outbreak, and took another sip of tea, smiling at Gulliver as if he was reciting a bedtime story to a child. "And what Columbus has to do with this is that Madsen figured that since ol' Chris Columbus had started this country, that would be a good enough day to collapse it."

"I thought you just said that Madsen had turned himself into a damn saint. That shit doesn't sound very saintly to me."

"Depends on who's looking at it. I'm willing to bet black people will find Mad-Dog's final act saintly."

Gulliver slapped himself upon the forehead in disbelief. "*Niggers?!* They're in on this to. Damn, what's next?"

"They own us now."

"What the fuck you say?"

"That's right, Gully. Niggers own us. Our buddy Madsen----"

"Oh no," Gulliver groaned. "No! No! No!"

Dudley nodded. "Madsen parceled the birth certificates out in blocks to certain, undisclosed African-Americans in this country, and since the debt is still outstanding, the documents are still redeemable." Dudley laughed glumly. "And come October, the shit will hit the fan."

Gulliver stood up defiantly. "Not if I can help it."

<<<<<<<<<<<<<<<

SOULFIRE BOOKS

<<<<<<<<<<<<<

The next morning when Gulliver saw that it was almost nine o'clock, he beat a hasty exit from his downtown office, and drove across to New Jersey to preview all the info Dudley had accumulated on Paul Madsen.

After reading over a few pages of the info, Gulliver smiled widely. "You've come through again, Bill."

"But with no solution," Dudley admitted. "The scheme is highly complex, extraordinarily well-conceived, and I'm not really sure what to expect of my banker friend. He has made it clear that he won't touch this unless there are no other options. As you can imagine, he's not going to be the bag man in this."

"How strong is his hand?"

"It's an iron fist. For starters, he doesn't need us. We need him. I don't know exactly how this fell into his lap, but the way he explains it is that Madsen was as shrewd as they came."

Dudley got up, his attention drawn to the whistling of the tea kettle. Walking back into the room, he aired his thoughts. "Madsen had vision, and he sure as hell resisted the pressure of ego because he was content to salt this away until long after he was dead and gone." Dudley dipped a dollop of honey into his teacup. "His mastery of the whole thing is pure genius. Even though he didn't have the foggiest notion who would be in the driver's seat when the scheme unfolded, he did establish a sort of financial genealogy for the transaction.

Gulliver didn't believe that.

"Year after year," Dudley said admiringly, "Mad-Dog would shuffle dummy accounts around among three of the most trusted bankers in England until he could decide which one was best-suited to play god with the real account. He had worked out some sort of evaluation grid to eliminate the weakest two, and then about three months before he died, he closed out the dummy accounts, but establishing the actual account with the banker who he trusted most." Dudley switched the cup of tea to his other hand and checked his watch. "In order for the system to work like a charm, the guy who inherited the account, upon the demise of the original banker, would have to be equally as trustworthy."

"Evidently," Gulliver scoffed, "the plan had a flaw, seeing how your banker friend---."

Dudley patiently reminded Gulliver once more that the Swiss banker had not committed to helping them access the account. "Don't waste time speculating, Gully, because we're not out of the woods yet simply because we got a whiff of what's going on, and on behalf of my friend, I attest to his integrity. He is not open to wrong-doing where his career is concerned. We merely lucked up due to his passion for my friendship."

Gulliver grunted.

"All told, Gully, my friend is the ideal person to handle the account, just as Madsen had it clocked. He knew that attached to every banker is his reputation and honor, and when one dies, great care would be taken to find a replacement who operated on the same curve. Anything less would panic customers."

Gulliver impatiently stirred his tea as he frowned at Dudley. "To tell the damned truth, I'm not real interested in knowing how fucking smart or shrewd Madsen was, I just want to know how do we get to the bottom of this shit he pulled, and to yank the plug before anyone gets hurt?"

Dudley was honest. "It won't be easy."

THREE

On Friday when Dudley drove into New York, he wished to prevent himself from feeling like he was heading into a Roman coliseum to be tossed to the lions, but the notion persisted. For almost a year, he had faithfully avoided any physical contact with the metropolis, and now that he was back, he desired a speedy end to the business at hand so he could hurriedly return to the comforts of Greenbriar Westlake.

In mid-town Manhattan, he handled a few routine business chores, and afterwards phoned ahead to give notice of his pending arrival. Leaving the glistening building, he decided not to take a direct route to his destination, but once he noticed the swollen, morning traffic, he changed his mind.

During the remainder of the ride, Dudley had nothing to hope for, but for Gulliver's sake evaded feeling doomed. Still, there was every reason to fear the worst, and he was too much of a pessimist to conceive of any way to pull a rabbit out of the hat. Not now. It was too late in the game.

Dudley met Gulliver at ten, and could instantly see that the young man was very worried, and it was for this very reason that he wished they didn't have to rely solely on each other. Admittedly, it was no exaggeration that they had ample resources, but nothing could undo Madsen's evil. He was convinced of that.

The third man in the room was David East, a sober man of a rough and straightforward nature who had never discovered a talent for tact. He spoke bluntly and considered it a weakness in others who didn't. East's swarthy complexion suggested a mid-eastern lineage, but no one knew for certain. What they did know, however, was that he was perhaps the foremost commercial litigator in New York. He also played a mean bass guitar.

At first, Dudley had made strong objections about bringing East into their talks, but Gulliver wouldn't hear otherwise, and had faxed East a copy of their report on Madsen so that he could take a look at it.

"It's solid," East announced matter-of-factly. "Solid as a rock."

At this point, Dudley wanted to introduce some argument, legal or otherwise, but he saw that the wind was already gone out of Gulliver's sails. His mood afterwards wouldn't be pretty, but maybe knowing this early that they were sunk might turn out to be a mixed blessing. This way, it would be easier to get him to liquidate all his assets and to get in the wind.

"What about legal necessity?"

"It was legal necessity that started the crisis in '33 which, in turn, has started the coming catastrophe." East spoke flatly.

Gulliver appeared frozen. "And you can't change that?"

East turned his drink round and round in his hands. "Shit, Gulliver, what do you want me to do, repeal the 14th Amendment or something?" When he saw the glimmer of hope in Gulliver's eyes, he set the glass down. "Whoa, man, I was only kidding so don't even think about it. In any event…." He paused, stuck in thought. "Hey, don't quote me on this, guys, but that could very well be your ticket. It would be risky as hell---."

"What!?" Gulliver demanded. "Spit it out, Dave."

"Repealing the 14th Amendment." East nodded approvingly at the genius of the idea. "Yeah, it's worth a look since that is the baby that gave citizenship to the slaves. Truly comprehensive little gem; resolute, courageous, everything an amendment should be, but yet it has a few wounds that the Founding Fathers didn't lick quite clean enough." East shrugged. "Who's to say it couldn't work."

Dudley interceded, looking at Gulliver. "Maybe he's not the man for the job. Now that I got my thinking cap on, I do recall a few things from school. In other words, I'm wondering why the big snow job about the 14th Amendment when there is the 13th Amendment." He pointed at East accusingly. "You do remember that one, don't you?"

East, instead of wilting under Dudley's gaze, grew combative. "Fuck the 13th Amendment."

"It freed the bastards, dammit."

"Look, Gulliver," East lectured, ignoring Dudley. "Freedom, in any country, is as worthless as spit. Unless the son-of-a-bitch inherits citizenship, the law does not have to recognize him or any claim he makes in a court of law." Irked by Dudley's criticism, his brilliant mind easily coughed up data. "Judge Roger Taney settled that score in the Dred Scott case when he said basically that a nigger has no rights that white men are bound to respect."

Gulliver was ready to celebrate. "Told you the boy was a goddamn legal whiz, Bill. This calls for a fucking drink."

"Back to the point I was making," East said, "the 13th is docile. A free nigger may be bothersome, but is only a threat when he has the weight of citizenship. If you take away the rights of citizenship from the darkies, in October when they attempt to stake a claim to the documents, a valid claim can be made against it in court. Thanks to the Supreme Court's ruling in Dred Scott, a non-citizen has no standing in our courts and without full citizenship to back their play, Madsen's documents will be as worthless as used toilet paper."

Splashing a shot of expensive bourbon into the glasses, Gulliver patted East on the back. "How much is this going to cost?"

<<<<<<<<<<<<<<<<
SOULFIRE BOOKS
<<<<<<<<<<<<<<<<<

Perhaps Jamal had tried to carry too much at one time, but when the clothing slipped out of his arms, the jewelry box crashed to the floor, and cracked open. He gasped and immediately dropped to his knees to inspect the damage.

"*Mama!*" Eric yelled. "*Come here!*"

Bernice Morris, a strikingly elegant black woman in her mid-forties, hurried over to see what the commotion was about. "What in the world is going on?"

"Mama," Eric shrieked. "Jamal cracked the jewelry box."

"I-I didn't know it was in the closet with my clothes." Jamal eyed his younger brother suspiciously. "How did it get there anyway?"

"Don't look at me, I---"

"Hush, you two," Bernice scolded. "I put it there."

Both Jamal and Eric were surprised. They both knew about the jewelry box, and when they were young had been told the box was magic, and that they should never touch it. They never had. The jewelry box had always sat on their mother's dresser, and was never moved.

"Bernice looked lovingly at her sons. "I hid it there when I had my room painted because I felt it would be safe there." She sighed. "I decided to leave it there."

"Why?" Jamal asked, "Granddaddy gave it to you."

Bernice sighed again. "But not to keep. Is it damaged badly? Give it here and let me see," Running her finger along the crack in the box, she could see that the break was not that severe, but her fear was. She remembered how stern her father had been when he had sworn her to secrecy, and had warned her not to say a mumbling word about the box. *Ever!* All she was supposed to do was too safeguard it, and then to pass it on. If she failed, she had been told, the whole family would die brutally. Bernice had never been more frightened in her life. "There is something both of you need to know. Let's talk."

It was naturally difficult for the brothers to believe what they were hearing, and to a considerable extent, it all sounded like a scene from an urban fairytale. What else in real life could follow such a bizarre pattern? No fantasy could have taken shape like this. A white Englishman, dying of tuberculosis, stumbles into a greasy spoon diner, and blesses the family with untold wealth.

"It just so happens that Grandpa Bernie was in the right place at the right time," Bernice offered, "and because of that, we have everything that we have. Your great-grandfather was the richest black man in the country, and our wealth started with that white stranger."

"But what does the jewelry box have to do with this?"

"All I know---, " Bernice began slowly. "All I know is that the white man, Mister Madsen, gave granddaddy the box." She paused.

"You still haven't told us about the box, Mama. Granddaddy had to tell you."

Bernice glanced at her sons. "He told me the same thing I'm going to tell you. Don't let anyone outside of this house know anything about this box."

"We already know that. We just want to know what's in it," Jamal prodded.

"Yeah, Mama, why can't we open it and see since it is already cracked?"

Bernice snatched the box off of the coffee table. "*No!*" she shrieked. She raced from the room, clutching the jewelry box to her bosom. "*No!*" she wailed mournfully.

Without speaking, the brothers hurried behind their mother, following her into the bedroom.

"What's wrong?' Jamal inquired. "What is it about that box?"

"Tell us, Mama," Eric interrupted. "What are you afraid of?"

Bernice pivoted, closed the bedroom door, and then for a second, stood paralyzed. It was evident she was terrified. "For a lot of reasons, I do not want to share with you our family burden, but I have no choice." She touched her finger to the box. "Just like my father and his father before him, I don't know what's in this box, but I'll tell you just like they were told, and like I was told." She began to weep softly. "If either of you try to find out what's inside the box, it will get us all killed."

"Wh-who told you that?" Jamal stuttered.

"That's what Mister Madsen told my grandfather and he was emphatic about it. Granddaddy was told to enjoy the wealth, but to keep the box a secret."

"And the white man---?"

"No. He never said what was inside the box. He just said that one day men, the president included, would want that box, and that they wouldn't hesitate to kill to get it."

"Oh my God." Eric groaned in panic.

Jamal glared at him shamefully. "Be cool, man. We haven't got anything to worry about if this stays quiet." He kissed his mother's cheek. "It's alright. The secret is safe. What did you say the white man's name was?"

"Paul Madsen. He was from London."

"This is not some sort of family prank you're playing on me because I'm going away to college, is it?"

No, Jamal, it isn't," Bernice said. "We owe every dime we have to Mister Madsen. Life before he came along was not so pretty."

Eric eyed the box. "Look at it. What could be that important, that small?"

"Documents," the mother admitted, " and that is all you need to know." She gathered her sons close to her. "Now, you have got to promise me that you will never say a word to anyone. Promise me," she demanded.

Eric spoke first. "I promise."

Bernice and Eric stared at Jamal.

"Why can't we just drop the box in the river, and get rid of it, once and for all?"

"No, Jamal," Bernice said sternly, "the box is never to leave this family. Now, promise me, son."

Jamal sighed. "I promise."

"Starting now, I'm entrusting the box to you boys. Eric, while Jamal is in college, you keep it." She thrust the cracked box into her younger son's hands. "Remember," she whispered, "our lives are in your care."

Eric fearfully studied the jewelry box, staring numbly at the ugly gash that now covered its front. Suddenly, the tiny box seemed to weigh a ton in his hands, so as a precaution, he gripped it tighter although he reeled at the responsibility. He was trained in living the good life, and fear triggered his desire to continue his life without having anything to do with the box. He extended the box to Jamal. "Here, take it with you."

"You listen to me!" Bernice exclaimed harshly, her voice urgent and demanding. "You will keep the box as I told you, and that is the end of the conversation. Now, finish helping your brother to pack."

FOUR

For the first time in his life, Jamal had to stand on his own, but college, he surprisingly found, posed no real problems for him. Even though his character had been forged in the lap of luxury, and his personality shaped under the most fortunate of circumstances, he was spirited and strong. Skilled in the martial arts, he could easily defend himself against any bully foolish enough to mistake his preppiness for weakness because once pushed into a situation where he had to strike, he could be deadly.

A fairly large number of his relatives swore he looked like his great-grandfather, but an equally large number insisted that it was Eric who resembled Bernie most. Either way, both of Bernice's sons were tall, dark, and handsome with almond-shaped brown eyes that hovered above a set of perfectly matched dimples on chocolate cheeks that opened wide when either of the boys smiled.

Having fallen in love with a computer geek, it was common for Jamal to spend his evenings with Venus in her off-campus studio apartment, watching her as she worked out the kinks in her new software. Usually, he was bored but would never confess it to Venus, who at 5'7" wore her mocha-colored skin so adorably well. Her hair was cut short into a small Afro and she loved wearing big, shiny earrings. She was, in fact, a modern-day Pam Grier.

"Give me a name," Venus ordered, hunched over her computer. "I want to see if this works." When Jamal didn't respond quickly enough, she urged him to participate. "Come on, sweetheart, I've spent hours on this program. Name one person who you don't know anything about, and let's see if I can---"

"Paul Madsen."

As soon as the words flew out of his mouth, Jamal wished he could recall them, and he silently cursed himself for his carelessness, but Venus' fingers were already happily tapping out the name.

"How's that last name spelled. M-A-D-S-E-N?"

"Forget it, Venus, I've changed my mind. Forget you ever heard that name."

"Don't be silly, Jamal," Venus scolded him, "and haven't I told you a thousand times to stop doubting my capabilities. You're forever beating the bushes, trying to find ways to keep me from reaching my goal." She laughed. "Well, you don't have to be easy on me because I've worked out all the kinks in this program, and I bet you dinner that I can find out anything I want to know about Paul Madsen."

And that was just what Jamal feared. The secrets of Paul Madsen were indistinguishable from the secrets of the jewelry box, so they needed to stay buried away, hidden. Too much depended on not knowing. The luxurious idleness of his family and their safety depended on this willful blindness, and all of a sudden, Jamal became a true realist. Everything that his mother had told him and his brother about the box, and what men would do to get it was real.

Oh my God, Jamal thought. What have I done?!

SOULFIRE BOOKS

On the last night of the month, the wind howled like a wild, wounded beast, and the snow that piled up in big, white heaps made it impossible to feel happy. Furthermore, all a sudden, Jamal seemed to understand little of what was happening between him and Venus. Lately, she had become too much of a trouble-shooter to suit him. She wanted to either fix or to fight the world, him included. Yet, he also blamed himself. He was not firm enough with her, but once or twice had come dangerously close to smacking her up. Still, there was more than enough of a physical attraction to keep him from too much displeasure with her since she really knew how to make up after they had had an argument. Oddly enough, though, the chance of a night of blissful making-up was apparently not on the agenda.

The moment he had walked into her apartment, Jamal could sense that Venus was spoiling for a fight. She hadn't calmed down at all.

"Still mad, Sugar-Baby," Jamal teased playfully, hoping to humor her.

"What do you think?" She was working at her computer as she talked. "And why do you ask?"

"Because I love you, that's why." He kissed the top of Venus' head.

Her body jerked rigid. "Stop!"

"Do you want me to leave, Venus?"

"See, that's what I'm talking about." Tears filled Venus' eyes "You won't stand up to your problems. You'd rather run away." She stood. "That's no way for a man to live his life, Jamal, because it's a jungle out there, and unless you become more of a fighter, the world is going to eat you alive."

"Just because I'm not from the hood doesn't mean I don't know how to protect myself. I can---"

"Can what, kick ass?" Venus stared at Jamal. "You think I don't know all about your martial arts training." She stuck her chin out proudly. "I probably know more about you than you even know about yourself."

"Venus," Jamal yelped heatedly, "what have you been doing, spying on me behind my back?"

"In case you've forgotten, I'm an intelligence expert, and it's not spying; it's called checking."

"No matter," Jamal sputtered angrily, "you had no right to go digging through my background. That's personal and I resent it."

"And just who in the hell do you think you're supposed to be that your history and background are off-limits?"

"As your boyfriend," Jamal said in a gentler tone, "what I tell you should be enough."

Venus laughed bitterly. "You guys are such big liars. I don't believe half the shit I hear coming from men."

Jamal felt betrayed. Venus had no right to delve into his privacy or his family background because it may be that, Jamal feared, she might learn more than she had bargained for. If they were to have any chance of a future together, he would have to steer her away from prying into his family's past. Yet it was equally possible that she may have already seen something that wasn't for her eyes. It may, nevertheless, be too late.

"I wish that you hadn't done that, Venus. How can I ever trust you again?" Jamal groaned pitifully. "Is that what you do to everyone you meet? Makes me wonder if I was your boyfriend or one of your study cases."

"Stop being a crybaby, Jamal. Please." She opened a desk drawer. "Here." She plopped a manila folder on the desk.

Jamal eyes the folder cautiously. "What's that?"

"Your file."

"*My file?!*" Jamal was angry. "Venus, you're crazy. You must really believe you're some sort of super-spy?"

"I'm not a spy. For your information, I'm a hacker." She beamed with pride. "Deal with that."

Jamal snatched up the folder angrily. "Don't be—"

"Forget you, Jamal," Venus answered, "but before you go, I have something else for you." She slammed a second folder on the desk. It was identical to the first one, only thicker.

"Wh-what is this," Jamal stammered, fear in his voice.

"Read it and weep," Venus replied curtly.

Jamal stepped forward menacingly. "I asked you a question, Venus. Now, answer it. *What's in that damn folder?!*"

"It's about Paul Madsen," Venus hissed as she moved out of the way.

"I thought I told you to forget you ever heard that name. Why did you do this, Venus?" He gripped both her wrists tightly, applying pressure. "I feel like---"

"Oww, Jamal. Stop. You're hurting me."

Jamal squeezed harder.

"*Oww!*"

Jamal released her wrists. "You shouldn't have done this, Venus, especially after I told you to leave it alone."

Venus rubbed her sore wrists. "Get out!" she screamed loudly. "Go and see what kind of bloodsucker Paul Madsen was. He was evil, just like you."

Jamal took a step forward.

"No wonder why your family is so filthy rich."

Jamal stopped in his tracks.

"That's right. I know. Once I traced your family roots, I found that there was no money until your great-grandfather, Bernie, but he was a damn cook, Jamal. How did, all of a sudden, he go from being penniless to being the----."

"Shut up, Venus," Jamal ordered. "You don't know what you're talking about, so just shut up."

"I don't, huh?" Venus retorted defiantly. "I knew that something very strange or very miraculous had to have happened to your great-granddaddy, and when there was the mention of a white benefactor, I immediately guessed that this was where Paul Madsen must've come in at. I thought about the way the mere mention of the name freaked you out, so I put it all together."

"I-I can't believe how you have betrayed me, Venus."

"Grow up, Jamal, for real. And I really, really think you need to read about Mister Madsen because your family money stinks with blood."

SOULFIRE BOOKS

Jamal was afraid, but he forced himself to deny it. Once he started reading the papers on Paul Madsen, he knew that from that point on, his life would never be the same. His dorm-mate was gone for the weekend, so he had the room to himself, but suddenly he didn't wish to be alone. Somehow he suspected that he shouldn't face the bogeyman of Paul Madsen without some type of support system.

At around midnight, though his fear was still understandable, his worst apprehensions were also stirred to life. He had to study the file, if for no other reason than because Venus had, and he felt compelled to know what it was that she had learned. He didn't dare ponder the consequences of what he'd have to do to her if the files had disclosed information that would be a threat to his family. He would kill Venus before he let her harbor any secrets, especially where the jewelry box was concerned. His blood ran cold. Did Venus know what the jewelry box contained? For her sake, he hoped not.

Flipping the folder open, Jamal experienced a fierce cruelty envelop him that was so alien to his nature, it initially gagged him, but he didn't try to turn the feeling off. Too much was now at stake, and if the cat was out of the bag, he would kill to protect his mother and brother. He took a big, deep breath. The time had come for him to enter the world of Paul Madsen.

Jamal vomited.

As he systematically examined Venus' file on Paul Madsen, all speculation about him being a Good Samaritan collapsed under the damning weight of his unholy evil. By virtue of all the dirty deeds he had committed against humanity, if there was such a thing as a band of demons, Paul Madsen would surely be one of them.

Jamal vomited a second time. So this was Paul Madsen? Unlike so many of the fireside stories told when he was young about the wonderful white man from England who was unquestionably sent by God to lift Grandpa Bernie up, and to set him on the straight road, the tale told by Venus' file was very different. As early as the first grade, he had heard the heart-warming saga of Mister Madsen and black Bernie, the greatest cook in the whole world.

Legend had it that Mister Madsen, who was very, very rich, had travelled the world in search of ambrosia, the food of the gods. He had dined in all the fancy eating places in France, but his palate had not been satisfied. He had travelled all over Europe, then through the Far East, and during World War Two had pursued his quest on remote islands, supping with indigenous people mostly unknown to the rest of civilization. Despite all of this, Paul Madsen's quest had not been fulfilled.

By 1942, when he had arrived in New York City on a freighter, he was a sad, dejected man, and what was even more heart-breaking was that he, of all people, had begun to doubt if ambrosia truly existed.

Jamal's grandfather had recounted to him numerous times how Mister Madsen had once or twice contemplated suicide, and how he would stand on empty street corners, yelling out to strangers to lead him to the man who could prepare ambrosia. Money served no real purpose, Paul Madsen had allegedly said, if it could not permit him to partake of the food on which the gods of Olympus feasted. He had prayed and prayed and prayed. He had experienced all the exquisite pleasures of the flesh, and had participated in every expensive past-time known to exist, but the one thing he wanted most continued to elude him. *Ambrosia.*

It had been told to Jamal over and over again how Mister Madsen, who controlled a fortune of millions of dollars, had cried out that he would give away his great wealth for one bite of ambrosia. And that was when destiny had led him to the small, simple diner where Bernie Morris worked as a cook.

The way Jamal remembered it told, it was as cold as hell that terribly dark night when Paul Madsen had stumbled in, shivering and tired from his long voyage. He had politely introduced himself to the owner, and then had requested sustenance. When asked his preference, Paul Madsen had looked around in apparent disgust at the little, greasy-spoon restaurant, and had told the owned to surprise him with something digestible.

The owner, Big Bob Thornton, stung by the insult, had gone back into the kitchen personally, and had ordered Bernie to cook up a storm, to prepare something special, and then with complete trust in Bernie's skill, had gone back out to humor Mister Madsen until his dish arrived.

As the story went, no one, dead or alive, knew exactly what manner of herbs and spices Bernie had used in his famous beef stew, but when Paul Madsen had tasted it, he had wept for joy. At last, he had tasted what he was sure was ambrosia.

Bullshit! Jamal realized. It had all been a fairytale.

<<<<<<<<<<<<<<<<<
SOULFIRE BOOKS
<<<<<<<<<<<<<<<<<

In actuality, Paul Madsen had been an esteemed member of the Illuminati, a group of ruthless men who wanted to control all the governments of the world.

The Illuminati was formed in 1776, and by the time Paul Madsen had joined, these guardians of capitalism had been toppling and controlling governments for one hundred and fifty years.

The Madsens were distantly related to the Queen of England on their maternal side, but via their paternal bloodline were powerful members of the Black Nobility, who had been among the first rank of dynastic families for over five hundred years.

Along with the Rothschilds, another prominent family of the ruling aristocracy, the Madsens owned most of the stock in The Bank of England, and since 1694, the presidency of the bank alternated between the two families. The bank gave both the Rothschilds and the Madsens the apparent ease they desired to control the lives of most Englishmen, but national control was not nearly enough for either family, so in 1713 when Gilligan Madsen was in charge of the bank, he proposed the biggest gamble either family had ever dared. He would bid for the most coveted prize the world offered at the time: the contract to import slaves.

Nonetheless, this was the riskiest venture the Bank of England had ever considered, and the Rothschilds, pointing to the financial failure of earlier contractors, wanted nothing to do with it, but the Madsens were stubborn. They would go it alone.

It turned out that the issue was so explosive that it split the two houses, the Rothschilds viewing it as a spectacular waste of capital while the Madsens argued that it was a godsend. In effect, a private tug-of-war ensued as the two families became even more estranged as one group, the Madsens switched their political allegiance to the Tory party while the Rothschilds and the bank remained loyal to the Whigs.

In 1714, the Madsen family while still remaining with the Bank of England, decided to enter the slave trading business as a family endeavor, and with money in hand established contact with Lord Concord, England's ambassador to Spain.

As fortune would have it, Lord Concord, who was a commercial genius, had made powerful friends with many well-connected noblemen in Madrid, and after secret talks with Jacobite leaders, he succeeded in securing the contract for the Madsens, who immediately established the family-owned South Sea Company. With a deliberate touch of disrespect, they located the company next door to the Bank of England, and hiring Peter Madsen as the company's first controller, they instantly looked to recoup the eight million pounds they had paid for the contract.

It was a special triumph for the Madsen family, and they beamed with pride at their enormous accomplishment even though a single ship had yet to leave port. Everyone in England made good of the affair, except the powerful Godsey family in Jamaica who opposed the idea. Before this, they had supplied slaves to Spain.

Jamal's head ached as he read the documents which were so plain-spoken, they seemed to come to life. The events were so clear, they seemed to jump off the page.

"Have you read the contract?" Robert Godsey asked the British envoy to Madrid?"

"Quite unscrupulous, if you ask me," the envoy replied with certainty. "Smacks of chicanery."

"What the hell do you expect?" Godsey spat. "After all, it's the bloody Madsens, and when is the last time those blokes turned over a square deal?"

The envoy nodded. "I can appreciate your alarm, but, as it goes, the deal is sealed, and to make matters a bit worse for you is that 25% of the stock in the Madsens' new trading company--."

"By George!" Godsey exploded, "there is always the means to end a deal, no matter how frigging good it is. You're over there,

so I'm sure there is something you can do. At least, get the bloody contract suspended for a year."

"And this evidently means a lot of you?" the envoy quipped slyly.

"Bloody hell yes," Godsey confessed. "In return for the three or four thousand slaves I send Spain, I net up to 250,000 pounds of silver and gold."

"Hmm," the envoy mused. "Very lucrative arrangement. Most attractive." He sipped from his drink. "Such matters, as the one you now suggest, must be handled with the utmost delicacy. I would have to be terribly discreet since I would never wish to anger such a powerful family as the Madsens."

"To hell with them."

The envoy put his drink aside. "How easy for you to say, however, I'm in no position to be as bold....or perhaps as foolish."

A groan went up from Godsey. "Get this damned contract fixed," he sighed, "and you'll be entitled to 6.5% of my profits--- "

"For how long?"

"Let's say ten years."

The envoy shook his head rigidly.

"Twenty?"

Another shake of the head.

"When, then?"

"Forever!"

SOULFIRE BOOKS

"And you didn't make this up?"

"Why would I do such a thing as that, Mister Madsen." The envoy casually sipped his drink. "I swear by what I have told you. The Godsey family has hired me in an, er, attempt, shall we say, to undermine your most lucrative contract with Spain."

Peter Madsen saw red, but with some difficulty calmed himself down. His family had worked hard to acquire the contract and it was indeed generous. Under the provisions, the Madsens via their South Sea Company would be required to supply Spain with five thousand slaves annually for a term of thirty years. The King of Spain would be rewarded with thirty thousand pieces of silver for every slave delivered, but, in return, all the ports of Spain would be open to the ships of the South Sea Company.

"I could lose much if something were to go wrong--."

"And to think how long it must have taken your family to put together such a deal." The envoy made a great show of sympathy, "The Godseys are such boors, but they do offer amazing gifts." The envoy smiled, "They have insured me for the rest of my life."

Peter Madsen laughed.

"What do you find so amusing?" the envoy inquired. "Why are you grinning?"

"Because," Peter Madsen said coldly, "your life ends today."

SOULFIRE BOOKS

Under a cloudless sky, the boats set sail for Jamaica. The men aboard used the time to go over the details of the plan Peter Madsen had devised for them, and just before daybreak, the officer-in-charge strolled from man to man, rousing them from their fitful sleep to brief them one final time. However, they knew precisely what was expected of them.

"Not one of the Godsey are to get out alive," the captain commanded in a stern voice of doom. "Not a single one."

At slightly before sunrise, the men huddled together outside the boats, only a hundred yards from the Godsey plantation. They waited, watching as the morning sun crept up on the horizon until, at last, the order was given.

"CHARGE!"

And as planned, not a single Godsey escaped.

SOULFIRE BOOKS

With no further opposition to their plans, the Madsen's South Sea Company launched its maiden voyage. Amidst great celebration and cheering from the Madsen family, a fourth of the fleet sailed to the Gold Coast, a fourth set sail for Senegambia, and the other ships *headed towards Mozambique, all with one goal in mind: to find Africans.*

The venture was a smashing success and the Madsens made a handsome profit. Now, all of a sudden, every financier in England wanted to buy a piece of stock, and when the Queen died the following year, her shares were quickly snatched up by King George I. The Prince of Wales bought shares as did the governor, and in short time all the notable politicians.

Within a few years, the ambitious Madsens with their treasury swollen had grown so powerful they embarked on a second gamble even more mind-boggling than their decision to enter the slave trade. Now, they wanted the entire market to themselves. It was a difficult decision, but once the Madsens made up their minds, there was no turning back, so when they voted to exclude all the other companies from the slave trade, they knew it would mean war. So what?!

Arrogance of this magnitude had never been witnessed, but the Madsens were unfazed by the sheer audacity of pushing aside all the old contractors---the Dutch, the Portuguese, the French—and by themselves supply the whole world with slaves. And virtually no one counted them out. As a matter of fact, South Sea Company stock soared as practically everyone in England cheered the Madsens on. To be a shareholder of stock in the South Sea Company was a mark of distinction, and the organization Who's who list included most of the members of the House of Commons, virtually every member in the House of Lords, the Swiss canton of Berne, as well as Sir Isaac Newton.

<<<<<<<<<<<<

SOULFIRE BOOKS

<<<<<<<<<<<<

Jamal was appalled at what he read. The Madsens were such brutes, he mused. They had everyone's blood on their hands. Jamal closed the manila folder, closed his eyes, but was too caught up in the lives of the Madsens to stop reading, and now he was anxious to learn about one Madsen in particular: Paul. He reopened the file.

By the time, Paul Madsen was born in 1882, America had begun to run up huge debts to both the Bank of England and the Bank of France, both of whom were partly controlled by the Madsen family. Large sums of money were diverted from both banks as the state governments of America competed with each other in costly building projects, all of which pleased the Madsens immensely.

Jamal continued to read, but when he saw the first mention of Paul Madsen, he jumped as though someone had struck a match to him. Again, the images were clear. Paul Madsen had been five.

"Grandpa, what is money good for?"

Anthony Madsen chuckled. "What is money good for? My boy, money is good for everything. You see, Paulie, money is like a magic wand."

"How?" Paul Madsen asked innocently. "With a magic wand, you just wave it like this," he made a flourishing pass over his head with his left hand, "and you can have anything you want."

"Same thing with money, my boy. It's the exact same thing. Wave enough of it around, and miracles happen." Anthony tousled his grandson's hair. "Just so you'll know, laddie, there are some fools about who claim, for some reason or another, that money is the root of all evil, but that's a lie. It's not money that is the root of all evil, it's the lack of the stuff that is the root of all evil. So don't you ever forget the difference, you hear me, boy?"

"Yes sir," Paul Madsen replied. "I hear and I won't forget. Are we rich, grandpa?"

Anthony sighed. "There is never enough, so don't let anyone fool you."

"Yes sir."

Anthony stooped down until he was nose to nose with his grandson. "Never let anyone else handle your money. It's yours so you shouldn't need anyone to protect it for you, but you have got to be strong, Paulie, because a man only deserves what he is strong enough to defend and to protect. That's just how it is, Paulie. Don't question it, just be strong. Another thing is that in any deal, you must always own everything. If you have partners outside of this family, either buy or cheat them out of their shares. The Madsens are the kings of the hill, and there is no room for anyone else, you hear me? You are a Madsen, so that means everything must be under your control. Everyone must be under your authority."

"Yes sir." Paul Madsen understood. That much would soon be evident.

When it came to learning the family business, Paul Madsen turned out to be a chip off the old block, and at the early age of sixteen was already an important figure in the banking industry. As a clerk, he had a keen eye for the numbers and his knowledge of how to turn a deal was considerable, but what was most applauded by his father was that the young Madsen was not ashamed to get tough on the poor when they couldn't make their payments. Still, Grandpa Anthony felt Paulie's technique could use a bit of refinement because as he explained it, only petty men dealt in extortion. The Madsens, instead relied on exploitation. It was, after all, more natural, but without gall and balls, the subtle difference would be missed.

In 1902 when Paul Madsen was tapped to manage the London branch of the family-controlled Bank of Scotland, it was characteristic of all the bankers of the time to try to keep up arrangements with the Americans, and he was no different, but Paul Madsen was far shrewder than the other foreign bankers. The others simply wanted America to owe them, Paul Madsen wanted to own America.

Weary of simply being a money-lender, Paul Madsen had inherited his family trait of wanting to influence and to control the policy of other countries, and since his father, grandfather, and other Madsen men, dating back to antiquity, had enjoyed remarkable success in stamping their personality on the governments of their choosing, he would not break with tradition. Thank God for America.

For years, though, the idea of controlling America puzzled Paul Madsen because the young country, although incurring immense debt, usually maintained a vibrant economy, and always managed to settle their accounts satisfactorily, keeping the wolves from the door.

Via the bank of England, America's primary borrowing source, the Madsens had excellent contacts throughout the country, but none were conveniently close enough to dictate policy. The only time a Madsen had affected policy in America was when Edward had drafted the constitution of Carolina, shortly after the state was founded. And that was in 1670. Paul Madsen's feathers were ruffled by this.

In 1912, Paul Madsen bitterly resented the fact that at thirty years of age, he had not accomplished nearly as much as the other Madsens had at that same age,

"What am I doing wrong, Poppa?" Paul had asked. "Why can't I distinguish myself from all the other bankers. I am a Madsen, yet I can't break away from the rest of the pack."

"You've done well at the bank."

"But when has it been enough for a Madsen to be nothing more than the head of the public treasury. I want to conquer worlds and to control governments just the same as you and grandpa.

The father chuckled brightly. "You're a Madsen, alright. It's in your blood to rule, but practically everything is taken."

Madsen shook his head. "There's still America,"

"So, there is," the father agreed. "So, there it is."

"I want it, Poppa," Paul Madsen arrogantly exclaimed as if he was referring to a piece of peppermint candy. "I want it."

Up to this point, the elder Madsen's policy for America had been to 'loan and collect', but if one on their own was now intent on something more popular, such as taking over, then that person deserved the full support of the family. No Madsen had ever been opposed to adventure or conquest.

"Taking over a government is not like taking a wife. It takes a little more time with a government," the father joked. "In any event, it is a process that we Madsens have perfected, and if you do as I'm going to tell you, then say, in about twenty years---"

"But that will be around 1933," Paul Madsen groaned.

"And I suppose that Rome was built in a day," his father remarked stiffly, "Plus, what is wrong with 1933?"

"Nothing, it's just that I—"

"1933, it is, then," the father interrupted. "That's your due date. If you're going to have a goal, you have to fix it with a due date just like in accounts receivable. Now, Paulie, there are two ways you can bring America under your iron fist within twenty years."

"How?"

"Taxes, for one. War, the other." The father stared his son directly in the eyes. "Choose your poison, son."

FIVE

What initially started as a dull throb at the base of his skull had soon progressed into a full-blown migraine, and Jamal sat up in bed, screaming in pain as all the tightly-packed nerves around his temples and eyes felt ready to explode. Troubled by the pain, he dashed to the bathroom and gobbled some pills, gulping some water although he was already convinced that this was no remedy. The pills were simply a meaningless gesture, a pharmaceutical salute to the temptation to be unrealistic because he knew damn well that the unpleasant experience he now faced derived from his suspicions and apprehensions about Paul Madsen. Clearly, he was overjoyed that he wouldn't have to kill Venus, but now, more than ever, he wanted to know what was inside the jewelry box.

And what of 1933? Jamal accepted the fact that he could never live peacefully with the big question mark shrouding his existence. He was certain that Paul Madsen had hatched a bold plan to take control of the country in 1933, but did he succeed? It just wasn't possible. America was America. Not Madsenville. But maybe the country wasn't named after Madsen for the same reason, whatever that was, that it wasn't named for Christopher Columbus. Now, that puzzled Jamal. If Columbus had discovered this country, why in the hell was it named after Amerigo Vespucci?

"Oh shit," Jamal gasped. "There were skeletons in the closet.

<<<<<<<<<<<<<<<

SOULFIRE BOOKS

<<<<<<<<<<<<<<<<

The following morning, a Tuesday, Gulliver carefully unpacked the mail delivered to his office via courier, and then spent the next five minutes worried about what the information would reveal. The stakes, by anyone's standards, were exceedingly high, but now with the prestige and authority of data from the Library of Congress in Washington, he had a scale on which to measure his speculations.

Gulliver phoned his secretary and informed her that he was not to be disturbed without it being a dire emergency. With that done, he phoned Dudley.

"It's here, Bill."

"What's wrong, you need instructions on how to open the envelope. Read the damned documents and call me back."

"1933," Gulliver grunted wearily. "Ready or not, here I come."

<<<<<<<<<<<<<<<<
SOULFIRE BOOKS
<<<<<<<<<<<<<<<<

Jamal buzzed about Venus' shoulder like an agitated bumble-bee.

"Good heavens, Jamal, sit down and be still. I can't concentrate with you in my ear like that. I want to be sure I get the right Library of Congress files."

A second later when she had gotten what she had sought, Jamal dashed back around to the desk, and stared at the screen. "Damn, that writing is tiny. What does the first sentence say?"

Venus read. "Since March 9th, 1933, the United States has been in a state of declared national emergency."

"What does that mean?"

"How do you think I know?" Venus retorted. She typed in some commands. "Let me try something else."

When a new screen appeared, Jamal blurted anxiously. "Is-it about Madsen?"

"No, Roosevelt."

"Who?"

"Franklin Roosevelt. He was the president that declared the state of national emergency----."

"Why," Jamal asked. "Find out why, Venus, but I bet it was because of Paul Madsen. He said that he was going to do something that year. Find out, Venus. Find out what he did. It had to be real big or bad if it made the president get scared like that. Wow!" Jamal exclaimed, "Paul Madsen was no joke. Damn, he made presidents tremble."

Once Venus had found what she was searching for, she emitted a startled gasp. "Oh my God, Jamal. It says right here that

Proclamation 2040 issued by President Roosevelt on March 9th, 1933, closed all the banks." She turned to Jamal. "Paul Madsen was a banker, so what does that tell you?"

Jamal shrugged. "I guess Paul Madsen caused something to happen. What, I don't know, but if the banks closed in 1933, you better believe that Paul Madsen was behind it. He had either done something or was about to do something."

Carefully studying the documents she had pulled up from the Library of Congress, Venus was struck by the irony of what Roosevelt had mentioned in his inaugural address on Match 4th, 1933, and what he actually did on the 9th. "I can't believe this shit."

"What? Did you find out what the emergency was?"

"Umm hmm," Venus mumbled. "It was The Great Depression, but what I find strange is why in the hell would Roosevelt close the banks when he knew people needed their money to buy food."

"Yeah," Jamal agreed, "that was cold. People needed to eat. Shit, if it had been me way back then, I would have kicked in the door at the bank and took my paper."

"There was no paper money back then, Mister Tough Guy. Everybody had gold, which, by the way, Roosevelt made everyone turn in."

"Not me. I wouldn't have fell for that bullshit. What kind of sense does that make? You're in a depression which is bad enough, but you've got to turn in your gold as well." Jamal shook his head. "I wouldn't have kicked out my gold."

"You had to, Jamal, or get fined $10,000. Either that, or you could go to jail for ten years."

"But what did they do with the gold?"

Venus studied another document. "It says right here that the gold was moved offshore---."

"*Offshore?!*" Jamal exclaimed loudly.

Venus spoke in a small voice. "Do you think that means what I think it means?"

Jamal nodded slowly.

"*Paul Madsen got it!*" they both shrieked.

SOULFIRE BOOKS

The truth was that the two men, Achton Levy and Gulliver, didn't particularly care for each other so Gulliver was mindful to set just the right tone for the hastily-arranged meeting in his office. It was important that Gulliver succeed in encouraging Levy to talk because if there was anyone with the intellectual energy to shed some light on the shit that Roosevelt had pulled back in '33, it was Levy, the leading historian in New York.

"So glad you could make it, Professor, " Gulliver said by way of greeting, welcoming Levy into his office and ushering him to a chair. "I hope your visit here won't pose much of an inconvenience. I realize how tight your schedule must be, so I'll be as brief as possible, but even then," he remarked candidly, holding Levy's unwavering gaze, "it may take some time." Gulliver sat. "I hope you understand."

"Yes, of course," Levy returned. "Your secretary was sure I got the impression that this was of the utmost importance."

"I'm in need of a scholar."

Levy nodded. "I'm delighted that you imagine me to be one. I'm charmed."

"This is serious, Professor," Gulliver protested.

"As I suspect most emergencies are." Levy grinned. "And yes, it is so good to see you again since I never had the opportunity to thank you for the lovely knife in the back. In fact---."

"Forget the past, Professor, because I just happen to know that there is a chair about to become vacant in the history department at a very prestigious university, and I'm in a position to, let me say, give you a five-star---."

"Aha, I see.'

"Not only that, but I know someone who would almost die to assist you in getting your papers published."

"Hmm," Levy mused, "and just what is the price tag of such superb concessions?"

When it turned out that Gulliver didn't require much in return for his enticements, Professor Levy felt exceptionally euphoric by his overwhelmingly good fortune. "And that is the long and the short of it?"

"Precisely."

"So, am I to understand it that all you request is information pertaining to history?"

"That's it," Gulliver commented flatly. "Not a damn thing more."

"Nothing?"

"Other than strict confidentiality, no. Nothing."

"The strictest confidentiality attaches to any conversation I have with others outside my profession, so you need not fear a word of this being repeated."

"Good, we understand each other."

Professor Levy clasped his hands in his lap and sank back into the soft contours of the chair. "Now that it appears we are agreed on all salient points, just what is it that you need to know?"

Gulliver licked his bottom lip nervously. "Just what the hell happened to the country in 1933?"

Professor Levy smiled. "Oh, that."

SOULFIRE BOOKS

When Jamal finished reading the 1933 Federal Reserve Board Resolution, he understood. "It wasn't the depression, Venus, that caused the so-called national emergency. It was the people wanting their money."

"Show me where it says that."

Jamal pointed as Venus read the section:

*"Resolution Adopted By The Federal
Reserve Board of New York. Whereas,
in the opinion of the Board of Directors of
New York, The continued and increasing
withdrawal of currency and gold from the
banks of the country has now created a national emergency . . . ."*

When Venus was through reading, she raised her eyes, frowning. "This doesn't sound good, Jamal, and it doesn't make good sense either." She pulled up an attachment. "More or less, the gold was seized, and then the army was brought in to protect the Federal Reserve."

"But what good would that do if the money was not there?"

"They were fronting, Jamal. The way I see it is that the government didn't want the people to know they were now broke, and that there was no money in the whole country."

"You mean the country was bankrupt?"

"Think, Jamal, sweetheart, if gold was the only currency, and all the gold was seized, and then shipped out of the country, what does that mean? It means, sweetheart, that with no gold, the country was bankrupt."

"I can't dispute that," Jamal protested, "but maybe Uncle Sam had some kind of collateral."

"Yeah, like what," Venus laughed.

<<<<<<<<<<<<<<<
SOULFIRE BOOKS
<<<<<<<<<<<<<<<

By 10:30, Gulliver no longer bothered interrupting Professor Levy with questions.

"From the middle of the eighteenth century, it was obviously clear that certain families in this country were operating in tandem with foreign investors to push this country into debt. Once this happened, the elite class would play a significant role in ruining and then running this country."

"But why?"

"Why not," Levy snapped. "Be mindful of the fact that most of these powerful families were not devoted American loyalists. Both their family origins and their family money had roots in another country, so America fascinated them only as a source of untapped wealth. These people were the allies and patrons of the banks they were connected to in their country of origin, so to them America was nothing more than a huge business, a corporation where they made money."

"These families----."

"We don't have to be abstract, Gulliver. I can name names. I can count heads starting with the old aristocracy of England and Europe all the way back to the 1700s up to some of your chums." The Professor crossed his long legs at the ankles and waved his slightly pale, well-manicured hands with shameless effrontery. He studied Gulliver critically. "I'm bound to inform you that this didn't start in 1933."

Gulliver grasped his head between his hands. "What now?"

"America does not exist!"

"*What?!*" Gulliver bolted upright in his chair. "And just what kind of fucking mumbo-jumbo is that. America doesn't exist."

"Well, let me be more precise. The government of America doesn't exist, at least not in the manner we were taught in civics class." When Gulliver attempted to confront that sentiment, there was one more effusive wave of the Professor's hand to silence him. "Hear me out before you start calling me the Anti-Christ. In any event, the 13th and 14th Amendments were the real culprits as they ushered in a brand new government which was at diverse ends from what the Founders intended."

"So what you're telling me is that the Founders of this country would have been against freeing the slaves? As I recall, that was what the 13th was all about."

"The bogus 13th Amendment of 1865, you must mean?"

"Bogus. Come on, Professor. Bogus?"

"Quite so. You see the original 13th Amendment was ratified by the states in 1891, and had nothing to do with slavery. At the time, the issue of white privilege was more of a concern than black servitude. It turned out that even then, foreign bankers were in cahoots to dictate policy in this country via politicians, and aware of the growing problem, the powers-that-be passed the original 13th Amendment which states in part that "*If any citizen of The United States shall accept, claim, receive or retain any title of nobility or honour, or shall, without the consent of Congress, accept and retain any present, pension, office or emolument of any kind whatever from any emperor, king, prince or foreign power, such person shall cease to be a citizen of The United States and shall be incapable of holding any office of trust or profit under them or either of them.* Quote, unquote," Levy stated wryly.

"And that was the original 13th Amendment?"

"Yes, and you see how it addresses quite openly the fear of politicians being swayed by foreign powers, but more subtly it attacked home-grown bankers who, due to greed, wouldn't hesitate to seek special privileges from abroad."

Gulliver scratched his chin thoughtfully. "I'm convinced there must be a simpler explanation for this country having two 13th Amendments."

Levy winced. "I hope you won't quarrel with me when I tell you there's only one. The first one was forgotten all too happily, and foreign bankers were waiting like vultures for it to happen."

"What about the 14th Amendment, then?"

"As you can imagine, the South was against the 14th Amendment, so the Northern Army unseated the southern legislatures literally at gunpoint, and put a puppet legislature in place that voted to ratify the amendment."

"And?"

"It established not citizenship, but privileges for a people now totally dependent upon the federal government which was quietly formed in Washington in 1871, three years after the forced ratification of the 14th Amendment. This marks the cut-off date of the real America government, and began the present era of corporate government, and that's what I was saying a while ago. The government of today is not the republican government that came into existence by the Constitution. All told, this whole shebang called democracy is a violation of law."

Although Gulliver had no extensive background in history, he knew that the Professor was not lying.

"But even as sensational as that little episode was, what was happening across the water in England was no less important because the bank of England smelled blood, and was ready to pounce on America like a hungry cheetah pounces on a too slow antelope." Levy asked for a glass of sherry. "You must understand that once the foreign investors had finally helped establish central banking in his country by way of the Bank of The United States, they wasted no time before they had the American bankers jumping through hoops." Levy took a swallow of sherry, savoring it. "If school wasn't such a crock of shit, you would have learned about a document called "The Hazard Circular." Levy grinned. "I don't know which is worse, The Lost Books of the Bible or the omitted texts from history. Nevertheless, when English bankers saw that slavery was about to be abolished, they were all for it."

"But wasn't slavery a bread-basket for them?"

"That's very true," Levy agreed, "but human slavery was old hat by then, the novelty and mystique long gone, so they had their sights set on another type of slavery. Economic slavery was to become the new money game."

"Economic servitude?"

"Yes. You see the English were too genteel for human bondage. Too much of a responsibility. You have to take care of slaves; you know, food, shelter, and such. To the English bankers, that was a bit much, so they opted for something with the same sort of financial rewards but without all the bother and fuss."

"And that is where this so-called Hazard Circular came in?"

"The Hazard Circular originated in England, and was distributed to all the bankers in America instructing them about the new gravy train. Owning labor, as in human bondage, was passé, they said. The in thing was not to own labor, but to control labor through the control of wages."

Gulliver had a worried look on his face. "How?"

"Simple. They felt they could control the value of money through a system called fractional reserve banking, but first all the paper money first issued by Lincoln, had to be taken out of circulation, and replaced with government bonds."

Gulliver unclasped his hands and drummed his fingers on the desk. "The English bastards knew they couldn't maintain any control of the greenbacks, but they could control the bonds."

"Of course since they would be the one who issued them. Once the Secretary of the Treasury fell in line, the Contraction Act was passed which allowed him to issue the bonds and then to retire all U.S. currency. As can be imagined, this Act allowed bankers to restrict and to control the amount of money in circulation at any given time. This way they could manipulate the economy, and many of them amassed huge grants of property like this. If they saw a piece of land they wanted, they would simply reduce the available money, and, in time, foreclose." Levy winked. "Ever heard the term 'robber baron' before?"

"Okay, okay," Gulliver wailed. "I'm convinced that bankers were the scum of the earth, but how does this all tie in---?"

Levy finished his drink. "I thought you'd never ask," he smiled, "but first another drink and one of those fine Cuban cigars I hear you keep on hand."

Abruptly, the ambiance of the room changed as crowds of curious thoughts and images exposed themselves in the back of Gulliver's mind, and then resumed their play. His blood ran cold and Gulliver, now more than ever, reckoned that he was soon to cross over into the hallowed precinct of Paul Madsen's evil.

What manner of man was this?

SOULFIRE BOOKS

The chatter in Venus' study died down as she and Jamal pored over the data on the screen of her computer, but they still were unable to locate the source of the country's debt. Assuming they would better be able to understand the situation if they knew how the country had gotten into debt to begin with, they scoured tons of documents from the Library of Congress. They were thinking of road repairs, better communications systems, and the like as well as money to build and maintain an army. Additionally, a country had to evolve businesses but all these expenditures were common, and wouldn't be any real cause of alarm, so it had to be something else that had swollen the national debt.

"Maybe those funky-looking, powdered wigs were really expensive," Venus joked,"

"Or maybe it was...." Jamal stopped, staring at the new document. "*Bingo!*" he yelled excitedly. "There it is!"

Venus looked backwards towards her boyfriend. "Where?"

Quiet pandemonium broke out as they read the document, absorbing the information, and then silently tossing it back and forth among themselves.

"You think---?" Venus started.

"Has to be."

They were both silent once more as they trained their eyes on the words again, and just as before, mutely presided over what the words represented.

"You still think---."

Jamal nodded his head. "Has to be."

"But this is unbelievable."

"It happened, though. In return for permission to cede a portion of Virginia, and an equal portion of Maryland to create the District of Columbia, the federal government agreed to absorb the debts of all the state governments."

"Wow," Venus commented, "so from day one, the federal government was in debt up to its neck." She paused. "And you know who they owed?"

Jamal knew. "Paul Madsen, and that was probably why he took all the gold."

SOULFIRE BOOKS

Others in a similar position would have called it quits, having heard enough, but not Gulliver. His entire way of life was being threatened so his need to know was immense. He knew of nothing that would permit him to turn away, so whatever this fresh report was that the Professor was about to make, he had to hear it. May God help him.

"Once everything was in place," Levy resumed, "the bankers were then ready for their amazing final act, and what a triumph it was. You had guys like JP Morgan and JD Rockefeller who were toeing the line for the Rothschilds while everything was coming together. At any rate, Congress got squeezed into the Credit Strengthening Act and when they did, all the nails were in the coffin. This Act awarded bankers the privilege to redeem the US Treasury bonds at face value. It was almost like getting money for nothing, and quicker than you could blink your eyes, the bankers possessed all the gold, but ultimately it belonged to the-----."

"Rothschilds?'

Levy shook his head. "I'm afraid not, Gulliver."

"But you said that the Rothschilds controlled the American bankers, didn't you?"

Levy smiled gamely. "Yes indeed, the Rothschilds did control the bankers, but the Madsens controlled the Rothschilds."

"So the Madsens got the gold?'

"Not all." Levy shrugged irritably, "but more than the lion's share." He sighed. "Yet everything Madsen had accomplished up to this point was merely the prelude to phase two."

"My God, phase two," Gulliver yelped. "The dirty, rotten scoundrel had masterminded the greatest banking conspiracy in the known world, and had stolen all the damned gold from his sister country while bankrupting the bitch in the process, and you mean to tell me that he wasn't finished yet?"

Levy nodded his head as if in apology. "Bankrupting America was not the definitive end Paul Madsen sought."

"Come on, Professor," Gulliver snorted. "What else was left?"

"Madsen didn't want to control the country, he wanted to own it---lock, stock and barrel."

Gulliver kept quiet about the birth certificates, owing to the fact that he had to see if Levy knew. "How in Christ's name did he intend to accomplish that?"

"How else? By staking a claim of ownership."

"To what, Professor," Gulliver ranted, "all property?"

"Think big, my friend. Think really big."

"*Big!?*" Gulliver scoffed. "What could be bigger than the ownership of property?"

"What about a fucking lien on your inalienable right?"

Gulliver groaned, shaking his head. "That's what I thought you'd say, dammit, but it's the last thing I needed to hear."

Levy eyed Gulliver suspiciously. "Then you must know?"

"Not everything, not even much of anything, but what I needed, I guess, was confirmation. This birth certificate shit--."

Levy stared at Gulliver threateningly. "Whether you want to hear any more or not, I still expect my chair."

"It's yours, dammit. Now, finish."

"As you wish." The Professor coughed delicately, fingering his empty glass. "Would you be so kind?" He handed the glass to Gulliver. "My vocal cords need loosening." Settling back with his drink, Levy got as comfortable as possible. "Madsen held all the trump cards, and simply played his hand. He knew America was powerless financially, so after the president was forced to declare bankruptcy in 1933, he let us stew in our embarrassment for a moment before getting the word out that he was up for discussions.

Congress jumped on the talks with both feet, but Madsen sent the representatives back home to discuss collateral."

"What was the deal? Gold for collateral?"

"Back in '33, all the governors of all the respective states held a behind-the-door meeting to cough up some collateral, but without the backing of gold, what could any of the governors bring to the table that would amount to a hill of beans?"

"And Madsen knew this?"

"Hell yes, he knew. This was his game, remember."

"So the governors put the people on the auction block?"

"Correct."

"But why would anyone want people as collateral?"

"You have to consider Paul Madsen to answer that. Despite all his foibles, he was like any other red-blooded member of an illustrious family. He had to prove himself. In order to be seen as successful, he had to be better than Papa, had to out-do Grandpa. Only thing was, he was a Madsen, a family proud of its slave-owning heritage, and Paul, the youngest male in the family, being the go-getter he was, probably desired to emulate the other great Madsen men."

"By owning other humans?"

Levy shrugged. "I'm no psychologist, but yes, I'd be very tempted to say that Paul, more than likely, suffered from a deep-rooted, unconscious need to do just that."

"What, own slaves?"

"Yes. You have to consider that for all his youth, he had probably reveled in all the grand tales of adventure and Madsen glory out on the high seas, battling pirates and the rolling waves to get to and from Africa with cargo after cargo of black gold. These true life sagas, no doubt, filled the boy with a tremendous sense of family pride, and developed in him a terrible wanderlust, not to mention the craving for fame and conquest."

"Be that as it may, how did Madsen pull this shit off? That's my question to you."

Levy appeared unperturbed by the outbreak. "Even once it was voted on that the people, as such, would stand as collateral to back the government's debt, there still existed a major snag. The state governments could only act in behalf of their residents in their personal capacity which meant, technically, that they lacked the vested authority to pledge individuals."

Gulliver grunted. "As if Madsen gave a flying fuck about our laws."

"He didn't, but to satisfy the constitutional mandate that no person could be held in bondage, it became imperative to forge a binding link between the human property and Paul Madsen, the creditor," Levy knocked back the rest of the drink. "What happened next was the deviously clever invention of the Straw Man."

"Straw Man?"

"You see, a Straw Man is a front used to accomplish some purpose not allowed otherwise. Keeping this in mind, when the governors made the pledge they, at the same time, consented to register the birth certificates of its citizens with the US Department of Commerce."

"And the damnable birth certificates became the collateral holding us, the people, in pledge."

"Paul Madsen, along with his Illuminati partners, held all the birth certificates as security. So now, you should realize why you pay taxes. Taxes on your home, your car, your wages. You are doing nothing but taking care of the governments' liability. The federal government got back its gold, and Paul Madsen owned our energy."

"Energy?"

"As in our energy to produce. The birth certificates are packaged in mass bulks, and today a single birth certificate is endorsed for one million dollars, that's up from about $600,000 back in '33. When a birth certificate is registered with The Department of Commerce, it is endorsed by no less than seventeen foreign nations. Sounds fantastic, I know, but it's true."

"Who has control of the birth certificates now?"

Levy shrugged. "Your guess is as good as mine on that, but whoever owns them can stake claim to not just us, but every damned thing we've produced. Just think, QuickSilver could be snatched right out from under your---?"

Gulliver shut Levy up. "No one is taking QuickSilver."

"But what could you---any of us---do. I don't believe anyone on the face of the earth knows what Madsen and his buddies did with their secured instruments. Even more scary is that no one knows just when their representative or agent is going to crawl up out of some hole with his fucking hands out. Gotcha," he'll say, "and we'll have to pay up. It's just that simple."

Gulliver, however, didn't hear that last part. He was too busy wondering what the weather was like in Switzerland.

SIX

The plane touched down with the force of a butterfly, and no sooner had they landed than Gulliver and Dudley whizzed off in a rental car to one of the luxury hotels in Zurich where after they had showered, shaved, and changed clothes, Dudley drove Gulliver to a second hotel.

Dudley glanced suspiciously at Gulliver. "Need I remind you that at this moment Herold is our ally, a most valuable one at that, so I caution you against spontaneous anger since we need my friend to get to first base. Again, Gulliver, Herold is a very dependable friend."

"Then I leave it up to you to get him to cooperate because where QuickSilver is concerned, I won't hesitate to assert my will by force if necessary."

"Just be an American darling and everything will be fine." Dudley pulled in front a beautiful building. "Well, my boy, here we are."

While crossing the hotel's lobby, Gulliver stopped Dudley just before they reached the elevator. He gripped Dudley's shoulder in a vise-like grip, a look of fear in his eyes. "I, for the most part, would prefer a cruel death with my body left to rot in the dirt than to allow any harm to come to the empire my father built."

Gulliver's meaning was clear.

"The only thing," Dudley said, "that's certain is that we won't accomplish a damned thing standing down here while Herold is up there."

"Let's go," Gulliver replied softly.

It turned out that Herold Pictet was not at all the rather old, pasty-faced wimp he'd expected, and since Gulliver was unused to being surprised, he cast a wary glance at Dudley. Herold Pictet didn't appear to be one accustomed to being pushed around or intimidated.

Dudley grinned sheepishly. He expected Gulliver to be momentarily put off by Herold's imposing physique and demeanor. Naturally, since he had never mentioned much about Herold the man, he assumed that Gulliver would conjure up a mental image completely different from what actually existed. Herold was in excellent physical condition, and had a well-earned reputation as a skilled mountain-climber. He was also an expert marksman.

After the introductions, Herold informed them that the room was soundproof, and said that he had taken the utmost care to ensure that no one knew of their meeting. "I would refuse to have come here without the guaranteed assurances that we could not speak with the undeniable confidence of not being overheard or monitored in any fashion." He came over with a tray of drinks. "I judged that every precaution should be taken."

"You judged rightly, my friend," Dudley conceded, "as this is a matter of great importance, not just to us---my friend and I---but to the whole country of America."

Gulliver permitted Dudley to lay out the preliminary formalities, but he couldn't help but notice how cold Herold's eyes were. They never twinkled or blinked, but were unwavering in their icy blankness.

"As much as possible," Dudley pleaded, "we need to be accommodated."

"I'm hardly surprised you feel this way," Herold confessed, "especially with both of you directly in the line of fire." He turned to Dudley. "You will have to excuse my forthrightness, but I must not have you mistake my friendship with you as a blanket zeal for Americans as a whole."

"Really?" Gulliver growled.

"I would have thought----"

"They don't call you guys ugly Americans without cause, Bill. You guys have wonderful rhetoric, and make such brilliant promises, but no one would be truly motivated to come to your rescue, if by chance, you tumbled into the mass grave you have dug for others."

Dudley was shocked. "And you really mean this, don't you?"

"Most certainly." Herold laughed gently. "Don't look so alarmed, my friend. I'm not a die-hard hater, but what assistance, if any, that I provide will be due to our friendship, and nothing more. If California and the rest of your beloved nation were to sink into your Pacific Ocean, I would not shed a tear."

"How much?" Gulliver snapped.

"See," Herold smiled at Dudley, "that's the attitude I deplore. Anyway, Bill, your timing could not be worse."

"And just what does that mean?" Gulliver cracked.

"It means that my hands are temporarily tied. Currently, the entire banking network here in under regulatory scrutiny."

"But isn't it true that Swiss banks operate with the strictest confidentiality?" Gulliver quipped.

"Which must not be confused with immunity or carte blanche to do as we very well please." Herold lit up a cigarette, taking a long, slow drag. "Right now, dozens of bankers and asset managers in Geneva are under investigation. Undoubtedly, Zurich is next. It appears that The Organization of Economic Cooperation and Development has adopted financial corruption as its pet cause, and not a single one of us is above suspicion."

"Okay," Gulliver rasped, "but that's not telling me a thing about my individual concern. Surely---"

"It should tell you," Herold butted in, "that it would be extremely dangerous for me to underestimate the full scope of the regulatory inquiry against my bank."

"So, what do you propose, Herold?"

"Not much more that I have already acknowledged, Bill, but nonetheless, a plum of a job is about to become open, and I'm on the short list as a possible candidate for the position."

Dudley sighed wearily. "What's the deal, Herold?"

Herold smashed out the cigarette, "In a deal worth 2.5 billion dollars, Deutshe Bank has agreed to purchase Scudder Investments. The announcement will be made next week."

"You want a fucking promotion," Gulliver spat. "Is that it?" He looked at Dudley. "Scudder, that's America, isn't it?"

Dudley nodded. "An asset management unit based here in Zurich."

Gulliver angrily snatched up the phone. "Kill that fucking deal, Bill."

"It may not be that simply, Gully."

"Why the hell not, I ask? With your inside track on every damned company at home, I'm sure you could show your friend here that he's playing with fire."

"Be my guest," Herold informed Dudley flippantly, "but whatever it is that your chum thinks you can do, wouldn't be enough as the deal is done."

Dudley put the phone aside. "And what does this mean to you?"

"As part of the deal, well, actually the deal will bring into being the fourth largest asset management service globally." Herold waved his hands around triumphantly. "And I could be named the chief executive. It's a wonderful opportunity, Bill."

Recognizing the predicament they were in, Dudley knew he had to move quickly. "Listen, Herold, I would never have dreamed of being put into a position where I would have no choice but to beg you to engage in wrongdoing, but this is what I am prepared to do."

Herold looked away. "That job I just mentioned?"

"It's yours," Gulliver offered grandly.

"What?"

"Yours," Gulliver re-emphasized. "You'll get the job. All you have to do is to stop being so fucking honest, and lose certain documents. Deal?"

Herold Pictet swooned, but immediately regained his composure. "I'll phone you tomorrow, my good American buddies."

<<<<<<<<<<<<<<<<<
SOULFIRE BOOKS
<<<<<<<<<<<<<<<<<

The next morning. Early.

Gulliver reached for the phone on the first ring. When the caller identified himself, Gulliver winked at Dudley. "Good morning, Herold. Wonderful news, I hope."

"I'm afraid not."

"What do you mean, you're afraid not?"

Dudley picked up on the other line. "Herold, what's up? Are you backing out of our deal? Why?"

"Bill," Herold explained, "I can't solve your problem."

"I'm confused, Bill. What are you saying?"

Herold sighed in resignation. "I checked the file on the documents, Bill, and guess what? There's another set of documents."

"What?!" Dudley exclaimed.

"Where?!" Gulliver roared.

"In your country. All I know is that Madsen gave the copy to a black cook. Go home. That's where you will find your answer. Bill."

"Yes, Herold."

"Godspeed, my beloved friend."

BOOK TWO

ONE

On the other hand, it suddenly dawned on both Jamal and Venus that what they had locked into was not the natural stuff of everyday tradition. This was scary. This was the kind of info that rarely found its way into the grasp of the common Joe or Jane, and both were wise enough to know the government would do anything necessary to prevent these documents from being publicly broadcast.

"Wow," Jamal gasped, "how many people know that?"

"What?'

"That international bankers control the Federal Reserve Bank, and that our tax dollars go to enrich them."

"Yeah, but the part that gets me," Venus huffed, "is that the constitution has been suspended since 1933, and no one bothered to tell us why we're still living under a state of declared emergency. And that shit about our birth certificates---."

Jamal shrugged. "Shit, Venus, you read what the attorney general said in 1973 when The Justice Department studied the feasibility of terminating The National Emergency Act. They were afraid to go back to the old way because the American people may not have known how to act without someone controlling them. The people had been conditioned to being regulated with all the licenses."

"But it would also mean the people wouldn't have to pay any more taxes. I bet Americans would know how to act with more money in their pockets."

"Of course, they would, baby-girl," Jamal teased, "but there was more to it than just giving power back to the people." He pointed at a document. "Re-read Senate Report 93-549 which is a congressional statement mentioning how futile it would be for them to try to put the declaration out of commission since the president won't cooperate."

"But why?"

"This would mean stripping the president of the extraordinary power granted him in a national emergency, and no president since Roosevelt has seen fit to deprive himself of this authority."

Fear showed on Venus' face. "You don't think the government will try to kill us if they ever found out we know about this stuff?"

"Naw," Jamal said consolingly, hugging his girlfriend. "They can't touch us if they don't know about us."

<<<<<<<<<<<<<<<
SOULFIRE BOOKS
<<<<<<<<<<<<<<<

For what it was worth, Gulliver knew he could mobilize huge armies of men, but how could he steer them on a straight course or to keep them on the beaten path when this was neither a typical right or left wing conspiracy? This time, it was a case of entirely different proportions; something almost otherworldly.

"Sometimes, I haven't got a clue as to which road I'm going to take." Gulliver spoke to Dudley, keeping his voice low. "I feel like a prostitute because it's like I'm working for someone else. Here I am busting my ass, and come October, I'll get the chance to meet my pimp, some nigger with his hands out, grinning." Gulliver shook his head, attempting to dispel that horrible image. "How unbelievable is that?" He bit his bottom lip. "At times, I feel like my best policy is a scorched earth campaign. Just destroy everything so that by October, there won't be a damned thing left. That's the thought I keep getting about nine out of ten times a fucking day."

Dudley understood. Things had indeed reached that point. Slowly, he pushed all the paper into a neat, single stack before stuffing them back into his briefcase. "These people are pretty good at finding out stuff."

"But isn't it unusual to take so long?"

"Based on the little info we gave them, I daresay two weeks is a long time. In any event, these guys are the best when it comes to information recovery."

Gulliver wondered what their win/loss record was.

"The guys are pros, Gully. As long as the records exist, they'll find them. It might take a little time, but these guys will crack the case. Trust me."

Gulliver cast a worried glance at Dudley. "You did give them the approval to kill, didn't you?'

"These guys are professionals of the highest order, Gully. They will acknowledge whatever needs to be done, and they will do it. I don't suspect they intend to drag this out, and nothing brings closure to a mission of this sort quicker than gunfire."

"Just how much do they know?"

"Enough to get the job done, but nothing about the particulars. It goes without saying that they had to be alert to what it was they were hunting for, but they were given no background."

"And you think they can do it?"

"These guys are good, Gully. Really good."

<<<<<<<<<<<<<<<<

SOULFIRE BOOKS

<<<<<<<<<<<<<<<

It had no doubt been clear to Barlow Gentry, a white, mid-aged, balding, gun-for-hire, for quite some time that it would be a waste of time to investigate all of New York's prominent, black families in search of a member who had been a cook in 1942. Such an approach would be unjustifiable, plus it carried too many impediments. The practice he had found to work to his advantage in a similar situation had been to work in reverse. He'd simply search the records for a cook that had sired a prominent family. This way was more reliable. If it was expected of him to find a nigger in the coal-yard, he felt the way to do it would be to wait until the nigger cleaned himself up. Gentry smiled to himself. No cook, no matter how much he loved frying bacon or scrambling eggs, would remain a cook very long after coming into an enormous pile of money. Not only would he quit his job, but he'd either get married or buy a car, and both big weddings and big cars left a god-awful paper trail.

Inasmuch as what he had discovered so far, it could be said with utmost certainty that the wealthiest black family in New York pre 1942 was the Matthews up on Striver's Row, but they were old money. They had ties with another well-known black family, the Greens, with whom they had owned and operated a string of funeral parlors throughout Harlem. For these two families, their riches were not prey to suspicion since their money had been amassed through hard work and diligence. He scratched them off his list.

Gentry pondered the fortunes of a few more black families in the register, but none struck his notice because most of their money had evolved from a combination of good business sense, and being in the right place at the right time.

Apart from these families, there were no other black families that had conceivably beat back the sting of poverty, but he did get the feeling that maybe he should pay closer attention to the Morris family when he conducted his double-check. Up on Sugar Hill, they had constituted new blood and no one in Harlem, moved up without leaving skeletons, unless Gentry surmised, they were George and Weezy Jefferson from the TV sitcom.

The Morris Family.

Hmmm?

SOULFIRE BOOKS

Gentry didn't feel like quibbling. "They're it, Dudley."

"And you're sure?"

"Everything fits like a fucking glove."

"The Morris family, huh?"

"Yep."

"Money?'

"They got it up the wazoo."

"Black cook?"

"Dudley, all of them are black, but, hell yes, there was a cook. Bernie, by name."

"Tell me about Bernie?"

"What's to tell. The whole family was as poor as church mice and then, all of a sudden, by New Year's Day 1943, they're not just nigger rich, Dudley. Shit, they were R-I-C-H with capital letters."

"Are you guys ready to----?"

"Just tell me what duties you need performed."

"Not on the phone," Dudley said. "Meet me at you-know-where in about thirty minutes. We'll talk then."

On the drive across town, Dudley managed to detach himself from the bloodshed he knew this meeting would call forth, and he hardly needed to remind himself of just how vicious Gentry was, but when you needed a whole family destroyed, there were no second choices. Barlow Gentry was your man. Dudley arrived first.

What followed the few seconds of silence after the men had seated themselves at the square table in the back of the auto repair shop, was a natural curiosity about each other's ulterior motives. Dudley, for his part, knew that men such as Gentry were not mere robots. They craved money and excitement.

Gentry was peering over the top of his stylish, designer glasses. "Whatever it is that you want done, I'd like to do it as quickly as possible."

"I'm only a sponsor---"

Gentry waved Dudley silent. "I don't recall asking in whose name you came. Do you have the cash?"

"Right here." Dudley hoisted an attaché case on top of the table. "There's extra," he shrugged. "This may not be typical."

"I imagine you will want this issue terminated to the fullest extent possible."

Dudley nodded impassively. "I want every true believer dead."

Gentry smiled, knowing that Dudley meant he wanted the entire family wiped out of existence."

"Case closed."

"Yeah, right." Gentry said, without bothering to look at Dudley, "but there's only one fucking thing wrong.'

"And what's that?" Dudley snarled.

"This is me, remember? The bastard you said you'd never fuck with again until the end of the world was near." Gentry started at Dudley. "No matter what, you have always kept your word, so I'm asking you, you bastard, is the end near?"

Dudley breathed heavily. "Not if you do your job."

TWO

If Venus would have arrived in the Chancellor's office a few seconds later, she would have not have heard the two men inquiring about Jamal. Immediately, her sharp intellect pieced together all the disjointed pieces of what she heard and then relating them to something sinister decided the men belonged to the other side.

As politely as possible, she mumbled an apology and exited the office, scooting down the hallway to Jamal's early morning accounting class.

Jamal seemed a bit agitated when he left the classroom. "Venus, the professor is—"

"They're here, Jamal."

"Who, Venus? What are you talking about?"

"The Secret Service or men like them were asking about you." Venus spoke rapidly, her voice inflated by anxiety. "In the office. I heard them."

"When?"

"Just now, Jamal. They're here." Venus gasped. "They know we were spying on them. Oh my God, Jamal, what do you think they are going to do to us?"

Jamal gripped Venus by the shoulder. "Calm down, girl."

Venus nodded, closely her eyes. "They're here, Jamal, and they've come to kill us."

"Let's go," Jamal commanded. "Right now, we know nothing." Still he wanted to go some place where it was certain he would be safe. Scrambling down the glossy hallway, tugging Venus along, he ripped out his cellphone, and frantically hit he speed dial button for home. *There was a fly in my soup today!* he howled into the phone in a fit of controlled panic.

"What was that about?" Venus asked curiously, struggling to keep up with Jamal. "A fly in what soup?"

"Don't worry," Jamal replied tensely. "They'll understand."

"Oh Lord!" Bernice Morris shrieked. *"Eric!"*

In response to Jamal's not-so-cryptic message, her heart beat like a drum. After all this time, her greatest fear had come to life, although it seemed so ludicrous that it would happen now, but when would be a good time to hear news that would turn your world upside down. Abruptly, life had turned ugly, and the vision was not pretty.

What had exposed them, she wondered as she stumbled through the house, trying to remember everything. As usual, she knew the danger.

"Eriiic! She screamed once more.

Without hesitation, her youngest son knew. "No!" he wailed. "Please, God, no."

"Get everything ready." Bernice's voice was firm. "Hurry."

Immediate evacuation was the first step of their emergency response plan, and both mother and son went about their duties efficiently, although they were terribly shaken. Bernice's father, in anticipation of just such a crisis, had formulated an emergency contingency escape plan for the family, but they had to move quickly. Ever since she had been twelve years old, her father had made her practice the Morris Emergency Plan as if it was a fire drill. He would sometimes rouse her from sleep yelling, 'there was a fly in my soup today', and pelt her legs with a leather belt if she was slow in responding. This, today, however was no drill. It was real. The mysterious men had finally arrived.

It was particularly important that they got out of the house within minutes, but she worried if Eric would remember everything she had taught him. Unfortunately, she didn't have time to voice her apprehensions. There was still much to do.

Breathing raggedly, Bernice raced to her in-home office, flicked on the computer, and steadily punched in a personal access code to an international bank account where, by rote, she transferred all the Morris money to a half-dozen smaller pre-arranged accounts. She took a few seconds to make sure all the transactions were finalized. That done, she raced to the library and quickly opened the hidden safe behind the portrait of her mother, and removed the stashed valuables, and the false identification cards.

"Eric!"

"I'm ready, Mama." Clutching the jewelry box, he darted down the steps behind his mother.

Downstairs in the den, Bernice went to another secured computer terminal, and flicking it on, compressed the built-in red button. When she released it, she sighed wearily. She had just erased the Morris family off the map. Plus, the house was programmed to explode in ten minutes.

Things would never be the same again.

SOULFIRE BOOKS

The first thing Gentry learned when he drove up to the mansion was that the Morris family had excellent taste. The home was beautiful, lavishly appointed with touches of a royal aristocracy.

The outside lawn was well-tended with bushes and shrubs which were neatly trimmed. There were even a pair of Mercedes Benzes in the carport.

Pulling up to the front door, he suppressed a laugh. "The good times are over. Surprise!"

In a flash, he and his men were inside the house, having kicked the front door off its hinges. "Round everybody up," Gentry commanded, "and bring them here. Now move!"

The men spread out over the house noiselessly, but just as Gentry started to head for the den, he noticed how the temperature of the house had skyrocketed, heating up like a furnace. There was something wrong, he surmised. Taking another step, he caught the vague whiff of what smelled like cordite. He stopped, then ran as fast as he could for the front portrait. He didn't have enough time to do anything but fling himself through the open doorway before the home exploded with a mighty roar.

Sitting dazed in a clump of bushes, Gentry swallowed hard as he saw the flames engulf the roof, and watched in stunned disbelief as a series of smaller explosions blew out the walls of the house.

Dragging himself back to his car, he noted that his men were dead, consumed by the smoke and fire, but after this brief acknowledgement, he found he was impressed by the spectacle he had just witnessed.

"Incredible!" he muttered to himself as he backed the car out of the driveway. "Fucking unbelievable." Driving down the highway, he was still astonished at what had just taken shape in his life, and suddenly he saw clear to the fact that this mission had much more strength and character than Dudley had alluded to. Or maybe Dudley had no idea of what he was up against. Gentry laughed bitterly. Influenced, perhaps by stereotype, Dudley had probably convinced himself that this would be a piece of cake. Gentry laughed again. If he was going to survive, he was going to have to think a little differently himself. Already he had acquired a deep respect for the Morris family. For one thing, they had served notice that he was not chasing Aunt Jemima or Uncle Ben, and the point was well taken.

THREE

On Wednesday, it rained like hell.

"You've got to stay, Venus."

"No," Venus screamed. "I'm going with you."

"Listen, girl," Jamal said testily, "you are in no danger. This is not about me and you."

"Then who is it about, then?"

"Me," Jamal sighed. "Me and my family."

Venus stared into Jamal's face searchingly, hunting for any signs of dishonesty, but when she saw nothing, she became angry. She shoved him backwards. "What is it that you haven't been telling me, Jamal, about your family? What have you gotten me into?"

"You're safe, so there is nothing else you need to know. This is about me and my family, and no one else, understand? So now go and live the rest of your life without worry. This is goodbye, girl." Jamal knew he had to destroy his relationship with Venus. He had to leave her, not just to protect her, but because to bring her along would be an innovation his family hadn't planned for. His family already knew what to do, how to act, how to disappear. Venus didn't. Even though it was hard to imagine a future without her, the situation was too critical for him to justify the side-effects her ignorance would bring. As for his family, they knew the drill, and now, for the first time, Jamal understood why they had been taught Spanish at a very early age. His father had scolded him countless times, telling him that once he had mastered the language, he would have the whole continent of South America to run to if the heat ever got too hot in the kitchen, Now, he understood.

"I thought we were always, Jamal?"

"Only if----."

"There you go, ready to run again.....as always." Venus sounded hurt. "What do you get out of running from your problems? I always thought that little boys were taught to be tough and to face their problems bravely." She embraced Jamal, snuggling up inside his embrace. "You don't have to run, Jamal."

What could he say?

"Or you could take me with you. One or the other is going to have to do." Venus stepped back. "So, what's it going to be?"

Jamal trudged slowly across the hotel room, thinking. He stared out of the large window with his back to Venus. "Order something from room service while I think this over." He spoke over his shoulder. "Pizza would be nice, but you can choose what kind."

Venus bristled. "Fuck food, Jamal. I need to know what's up, and I want to know now." She stormed across the room to stand beside him. "And yeah, I take back what I said a minute ago about going with you because I don't want to be with a coward."

The stinging rebuke disturbed Jamal. "You have never faced a situation like this before. It's not like going to a pep rally, if that's what you're thinking."

"And how in the hell do you know how big it is if you never stand up to it?"

It meant a lot to Jamal that Venus not think he was a coward, and he was fascinated by her determination to stand with him, but did he have the right to drag her into his troubles? For the moment, she was an outsider, and at present, that was where all the advantages were.

"Are you a man…or a mouse?" Venus taunted.

"And just who the hell do you think you are," Jamal blurted, "Superwoman, Xena, or one of Charlie's Angels?"

"None of those bitches," Venus hissed, "but I'm woman enough to stand by my man through thick and thin. Does that answer your damn question, Jamal?"

"Grab your hat and coat."

"Uh-oh, Jamal. I' not running."

"Shut up, Venus. I'm not running. I'm going to say goodbye to my family."

SOULFIRE BOOKS

Bernice and Eric spent their first day in hiding, waiting on Jamal to show up, and though both were worried about him, neither of the pair wished to go against the rules they were now forced to abide by. Sadly enough, their new way of doing things compelled them to abandon this place, the safe house, within 48 hours.

Part of the tradition, as far back as she could remember, was that at the earliest possible time after 'the fly in the soup' warning had been issued, the family was to assemble, from wherever they were, at the safe house. After 48 hours, they were to be out of the country.

Bernice was intent on observing the stiff formality of the emergency plan though it meant leaving her oldest son, so she prepared herself for that eventuality. Nevertheless, Jamal would know what to do if left behind. Thank God for Plan B. Still, why hadn't he phoned? In this type of situation, phoning home was more than a mere courtesy. It was a matter of life and death.

"Thank God!" Bernice shrieked from her post by the window when she saw Jamal drive up. The mysterious men had not gotten him after all. "Thank you, Jesus," she gratefully exclaimed. "Go let your brother in, Eric."

"Who's that girl with him?"

"Just go open the door." Bernice was too happy to care, yet she did unconsciously interpret the young girl as trouble or at least a burden. The girl didn't know, could never understand, and would never cease to be an outsider. In other words, this was the other side of the coin and no place for puppy love or holding hands. Bernice ascribed better sense to Jamal, but why in the devil's name did he bring the girl?

"Why didn't you call?" Eric pouted. "Had Mama worried to death."

"I'm fine, Mama."

"I see that now, but you--."

"Mama. Eric. This is Venus."

"Hello, Venus," Bernice said politely before turning to Jamal. "We are not gathered here for a family reunion, son. I don't understand."

"Everything is under control."

Bernice stared at Venus, feeling she was the reason Jamal was putting on this act of bravery, and she was not about to let him continue with his pretensions. "Are you crazy, boy? This is no college prank." She turned to Venus. "Sweetheart, please don't think this has anything to do with you, but Jamal---."

"She knows, Mama."

Bernice gasped. *"What?!"*

"She's the one who told me about the men hunting for me at school. Mama, please---."

"This was a family matter, Jamal. No one was supposed to know. How could you?"

"She will be family soon, Mama. This is your future daughter-in-law."

Bernice broke down and cried. "Boy, what have you done?"

Jamal comforted his smother. "It's going to be okay, Moms. I promise."

"What's done is done, I imagine," Bernice said, wiping her eyes. "We better make all necessary arrangements so we can leave on time."

"I'm not going, Mama."

"Not going, Jamal. You have to go. You know that. We all have to go. The mysterious men, Jamal."

"You and Eric go ahead. I'm---"

"No the hell you're not either, Jamal, so you might as well quit this foolishness because you're coming with us to south America, and I don't want to hear any more about it."

"I'm sorry, Mama, but I'm not running. I'm staying to fight."

Bernice laughed grimly. "Fight? Who......and how?" She faced Venus squarely. "Miss, I surely hope you're not the one responsible for filling Jamal's head up with this nonsense because it will only get him killed. You too."

"The decision to stay is my own," Jamal said defensively.

"And I guess it is also your decision to declare war on the mysterious men," Bernice huffed angrily.

"Mama, please listen." Jamal had never openly opposed his other before, but this was one occasion where he wanted to speak his mind. "Mama, listen, all our lives we have had to endure this great burden, knowing that one day the men might come. I know we all prayed they would never find us out, but they have."

"And you think you can beat them with one of your karate chops or something?"

Jamal sighed wearily. "You don't have time for me to bring you up on how it all works, but I think I can get them off our backs."

Bernice looked at Venus.

"I think so to, Mrs. Morris. I promise to take good care of him."

"But you're just a child yourself." Bernice shook her head. "I-I don't know about this, Jamal."

"I have an uncle who is a member of the Congressional Black Caucus---

"And you think the CBC can stop the mysterious men?"

"You have got to stop thinking of them as mystery men, Mama," Jamal pleaded. "That's why they seem so frightening. They're no mystery, Mama. They're men from the government more than likely or at least thugs hired by bankers. Anyway, I'm staying."

"Are you sure about this, Jamal?"

"I'm sure, Mama. I owe it to the family."

"But why? We're still just as rich as before, only now we're Spanish."

"I'll be okay, Mama."

Bernice hugged her son. "Please be careful."

Jamal nodded. "Where's the jewelry box?"

"In my bag," Eric replied.

"Give it here and let's find out what this is all about."

"No!" Bernice gasped. "Wait until I'm gone. I've gone this long without knowing, and I don't want to know now. Just promise me that you'll be careful."

"I promise, Mama. Now, go." Jamal hugged his mother and brother again. "I'll stay here until I hear from you, so call me as soon as you reach the villa."

SOULFIRE BOOKS

Jamal head pounded. "So this is what they're after." The jewelry box had been opened. "No wonder."

Venus was equally flabbergasted. "Wow!"

"I-I can't believe this," Jamal gasped. "It's just too far beyond my imagination. After all these years, now I know. Damn, what a secret."

"Jamal, sweetheart," Venus said, shaking her head. "It's not a secret anymore. Remember the men?"

"Who do you think sent them?"

"What difference does it make? Their objective is the same. They want those documents, Jamal, and they want them bad because they know that if they don't get them, your family will own….America. My God!"

"And I'm going to make you the Queen."

"Stop fooling around, Jamal, because this is bigger than I thought. We had better see what my uncle has to say about this. It is evident that we are going to need all the help we can get."

Jamal didn't argue.

<<<<<<<<<<<<<<<<
SOULFIRE BOOKS
<<<<<<<<<<<<<<<<<

Gentry's basic view of everything had changed. He usually adhered to the policy that as long as he stayed two steps ahead of the devil, he was one up on everyone else, but now he wasn't so sure. There were too many unexplainable loose ends, and just what was he to make of that bullshit with the Morris family? Damn, that still had his head spinning. One minute they were there, then POOF, they were gone, vanished like they had never even existed.

Even though he recognized he'd been outwitted, and that his efforts up to this point had proved worthless, he wasn't about to quit. Now, more than ever he had to know what this was all about. Completely. Totally. *Absolutely.*

Gentry did not allow himself to be alarmed that he was about to cross the line. It didn't matter. If there was any prospect of him getting any closer to the bottom of this mission, he had to know everything. After that near fiasco at the Morris home, it would be unthinkable for him to continue his pursuit without being fully apprised of every valid piece of data available, and since Dudley wouldn't give it to him, he would steal it.

He hated neighborhood snoops, so he decided to park the car down the street. He couldn't risk some busybody taking the tag number and reporting it to the cops. He crossed into the New Jersey complex where Dudley lived, and tried to make himself as invisible as possible as he mumbled into a small microphone fitted into the lapel of his pea coat. "Is everything ready?"

"Roger, we're all set."

"Good," Gentry replied.

"Any particular spot?"

"Half a block from the house would be perfect. I'll need the cover to draw attention away from the target area for a few minutes."

"How long you gonna need?"

"That's not certain. Either way, I'm out in twenty minutes, with or without what I came for. You copy?"

"Roger."

"Now, put on a good show."

Slipping into the darkness, and moving quickly in the direction of Dudley's home, Gentry looked over his shoulder in time to see a car pulling up sharply around the corner, and peeking over his other shoulder, he noticed another car barreling down the opposite end of the street, moving fast. Gentry smiled. That should make for a pretty good crash.

A second later when the cars collided, it caused such a loud noise it even made Gentry flinch, but he didn't stop running. These guys were professional stunt drivers who knew exactly what they were doing. He now had his cover, but from this point on, he was on his own.

At first the lock on Dudley's front door felt a bit overpowering, but Gentry understood that every lock had a different feel, and after a few seconds yanking at the lock's control mechanism, he segued into a gentle rocking chair motion that tripped the gadget open. Just before pushing into the house, he gazed at the staged spectacle down the street. He was covered. No one was looking in his direction. Everyone was too busy gawking at the driver of one of the cars who was on fire. Some of the bystanders were trying to douse the flames.

"Works for me," Gentry grunted as he entered Dudley's empty home. Glancing around to get his bearings, he turned zen-like, his attention focused. "It's show-time," he breathed almost wordlessly as he zeroed in on the study, figuring it was as good a place as any to concentrate his search.

Gentry tiptoed through the house with the stylish grace of a cat, a time-worn ballet where both of his feet had been programmed to make no noise. Entering the study, he moved blindingly quick his well-trained hands moving, touching, probing as his eyes scanned and missed nothing. Every movement, however slight, spoke of his special search skills, and Gentry understood the unspoken language of hiding places, and he respected their cold, unseeing demeanor. To him, the hunt for hidden objects was as passionate as the search for a woman's g-spot, and he used all his senses like radar. Unleashing himself into someone else's private space turned him on and with machine-like precision, he floated around like a ghost. So far, no one had ever hidden anything from him, and he doubted that someone--- no matter who---could hide something---anything---from him.

In ten minutes, he had found what he had come for.

SOULFIRE BOOKS

Later the same day.

By the end of the hour, Gentry had turned a whiter shade of pale.

"Damn!" he cursed before slumping back into the soft contours of his recliner. It took him a second or two to recover totally from his shock, but he looked at the documents once more and whistled shrilly. "Whew! If this doesn't take the damn cake, I don't know what the fuck does. *Whooeeee!"*

Since he was alone, he continued to whoop and holler for a few seconds more. Sure, he realized he probably looked pretty silly, but so what? He deserved it. Usually, after one of his successful missions, he'd simply acknowledge it as nothing more than another day at the office. He would then move on without so much as a drink or a congratulatory pat on the back, but not this time because despite his extensive training, he had never been taught how to handle what amounted to all of God's blessing in a single basket.

WOW!

Suddenly, it angered Gentry that Dudley had tried to keep something away from him this big. Gentry now despised the fact that Dudley intended to keep him neutralized while all the time keeping him in the dark about what was truly going on. Well, two could play that game.

FOUR

Congressman Peterson stood up stiffly, but since there was no place to go, he simply walked around in a complete circle. At the far end of the loop, he strung the imaginary oval out, and shuffled away in a heavy two-step. He refused to look at either his niece, Venus, or her boyfriend. He was still too stunned to speak. These were such extraordinary documents, so precise, so damned frightening.

The Constitution suspended? That was about as acceptable as believing that the American people had been put up as collateral to satisfy this country's debt. Peterson grimaced. He was no dummy, but it was still difficult to view himself and the rest of the population as pawn shop items.

"So, Uncle Willie, what do you think?"

Congressman Peterson fixed Venus and Jamal with an icy glare. "If word of this was picked up by the wrong ears, do you know what would happen?"

Both nodded.

"It wouldn't be pretty," Peterson remarked. "This is perhaps the biggest threat white America has ever faced, and I shudder at the thought of what they might do with their future in jeopardy." Peterson remembered Rosewood, the incident at Fort Pillow, Tennessee, and in his mind's eye could vividly see dark, black bodies swaying from southern trees. "It wouldn't be pretty," he repeated sadly. "This is the Apocalypse."

"I'm not sure I understand," Jamal admitted.

"What's not to understand, son, and while I commend you and your family for recognizing the gravity of this situation, what sort of restraint do you think we can expect from the others come October when the certificates are distributed? Suppose some dirt poor farmer down in Mississippi got one, say awarding him ownership of a big tobacco company. Do you think he is going to consider anything except his good luck?" Peterson grunted. "Nothing would be able to stop black folks from staking their claims. Almost overnight, you're going to have black folk, who just the night before, didn't have a boot to piss in, suddenly finding themselves CEOs and captains of industry." Peterson stared at his young guests. "And do you think white America is just going to accept that? Right now, I feel that our best chance of riding this out is to pray that the documents in the Swiss bank accounts are discovered."

"But that---." Venus began.

"I know, I know," Peterson grumbled, waving away the question. "Sure, this would put all the pressure on your boyfriend and his family, but it would be a whole lot easier to hide and to protect one family than it would be to hide and to protect every black man, woman, and child in this country."

"So, what you're saying, I believe," Jamal replied tightly, "is that you're very unsympathetic to my family. All of a sudden, we're expendable, right?"

"Jamal!" Venus cried. "I'm surprised at you. I'm sure my uncle didn't---."

"Let him answer," Jamal informed Venus. "Your uncle doesn't need a go-between. Go ahead, Mister Peterson, answer my question."

The tall, dark man who resembled Venus a lot spoke calmly. "First off, no black person is expendable, and I respect your concern for your family. Still, I think it would work best if the secret account in Switzerland is discovered because that would eliminate the chaos of black people looking to get paid come October. At least your family understands the risks so I feel it would be to our advantage if we leaked the information ourselves. This way mayhem will be averted in October."

"No," Jamal said firmly.

"Just what do you think would happen come October if, according to his instructions, the Swiss banker handling the account, went ahead and secretly funneled the birth certificates into this country, and then parceled them out to black organizations, charities or individuals as he deemed appropriate. Can you possibly imagine what these crackers would do once they had sufficiently recovered from their initial shock and astonishment?" Peterson winced. "It will be worse than the Holocaust."

"Oh God," Venus shrieked.

Peterson nodded, acknowledging the response. "According to the documents you have acquired, all hell is fixing to break loose in October unless we find some way to contain it."

"How," Venus asked. "The jewelry box contained clear instruction on where Paul Madsen had stored documents independent of each other so they could be cross-referenced for authenticity. Only one set of documents was stored in this country, the rest overseas, but upon our request and with the cover letter Paul Madsen had drawn up, all the info was mailed to an address of our choosing without any delay. In most cases, the documents arrived overnight."

"And you have all this paperwork?"

"It's put up," Jamal snapped.

"I see." Peterson glanced at Jamal. "Please understand me, son. I'm not the least bit interested in stealing your information, but the bottom line is that at some point, everything is going to have to be studied and analyzed." There was sadness in his eyes when he continued. "No offense, but no one is going to accept the word of two college students----.'

"No one is getting their hands on shit," Jamal cracked.

"In that case," Peterson said softly, "come back when you grow up."

FIVE

"He's gone!" Savoy Brown yelled into his walkie-talkie.

It was late afternoon, and Gentry raced out of the shadows until he reached his car. Screaming into the car phone, he ordered the two men in the black sedan to move into an intercept position at the next corner. "Quickly!" he commanded gruffly. "I want that bastard."

Gentry sped around the block, babbling hysterically to Brown who he had picked up from his checkpoint.

"He can't be far." Brown offered defensively.

"Are you crazy? This fucking family seems to possess the fucking power to disappear at will."

"We'll get him. He was only out of my sight for a second."

"Talk is cheap," Gentry uttered spitefully.

"We'll get him," Brown said again. "It's just one of those things that happen."

"Dammit, that wasn't supposed to happen. We can't afford to let this kid get in a position where he can initiate trouble. He may---."

"There he is!"

Just as Gentry was about to floor the car, the pair of men in the intercept vehicle rushed forward, trapping the young man like he was a hunted animal. Gentry leaned back in the car, breathing heavily. It wasn't enough that his men had their quarry hemmed in. "All right, you bastards," he mumbled softly to himself, "get him into the car. Yeah, yeah, good. Very fucking good." Gentry kept up the garbled commentary until the boy was wrestled into the backseat of the waiting car. "Right now, I want some answers."

It wasn't necessarily a long drive to the sterile house on the outskirts of town, but once they arrived, Gentry was eager to begin the interrogation.

"This will only take a few minutes of your time, Mister Morris," Gentry rasped, "but first we must verify your identity. Now, you can either cooperate or I'll cut your finger off in order to get a print. You do understand that I'm not kidding around, don't you?"

The frightened black teenager nodded rigidly.

Gentry patted the boy's cheek. "We're off to a good start. " He turned to one of his goons. "Take the gag off."

"My-my name is not Morris, sir," the boy stammered, his voice filled with fear. "My name is-----."

Gentry grinned. "Good try, Jamal. Now if you don't mind. I'd like to get a fingerprint. How about that, huh, Jamal?"

"Jamal? I don't know no Jamal Morris."

"Fingerprint him."

Brown marched the boy stiffly over to a makeshift countertop where the fingerprint equipment was set up. Brown roughly grabbed the boy's finger. "Relax or I'll break it." Extending the finger straight out, he smashed the upper portion of the digit into a smudge of black, gooey ink, and then pressed it deep onto a blank, white card. "Now, go sit the fuck down."

Brown walked over to a tight, wood door through to another secured area where a computer sat in the middle of an oblong Formica table. After he had switched the machine on, he listened contentedly to the hushed whir of the computer, and then seated himself with the confidence of someone who knew what he was doing.

With his back to the others, he tapped in an access code, and shortly thereafter slipped the fingerprint into the slot for transmittal. "This shouldn't take long," he casually informed Gentry.

"Do you wish to tell me who you are?" Gentry questioned the young, black man, "or do you insist on being found out. Your prints will certainly confirm our suspicions, Mister Morris.'

"I am not, my name is not Morris. I am---."

"Never mind him," Brown butted in, "here's the read-out."

Like a hungry vulture, Gentry hovered over the computer, anticipation rabid on his face. He glanced quickly over his shoulder. "This will spell out who you are, Jamal, and then I'm going to get a little tougher....*What?!*"

Both Gentry and Brown stared at the screen in utter disbelief. "What the fuck?!"

"James Toney," Gentry read.

"That's me," the young boy said weakly. "Told you my name wasn't no Jamal Morris. I ain't never even heard of that dude, man."

Feeling somehow that he'd been cheated again, Gentry barked at Brown. "You sure you didn't screw up?"

Sensing Gentry's bitterness, Brown ran the print again. *Same results.*

This time Gentry pretended not to be offended by his apparent error. He had mistaken James Toney for Jamal Morris. He studied the photo he had of Jamal Morris, the one taken with members of the college track team, and he placed it gingerly next to the picture on the computer screen of James Toney. The resemblance was remarkable.

"Give him some money," Gentry said apologetically, "and give him a ride to wherever he wants to go." He winked at Brown who know what that meant. It signified that James Toney had come to the end of the road.

"As you wish," Brown replied.

"Be quick about it," Gentry cracked. "The night is still young."

SOULFIRE BOOKS

'Round Midnight.

When the door came crashing down, the pencil-thin, young, white college freshman looked up, startled.

Gentry stepped across the splintered door with his gun drawn. "I don't have time to play fucking games with you." He pressed the gun into the boy's temple. "Where the fuck is Jamal Morris?"

"Gone," the boy yelped in panic. "That's all I know."

"Is that your final answer?"

"I don't know. I swear."

Gentry squeezed the trigger.

SOULFIRE BOOKS

Tommy York's plane landed on time. He scrambled through the bustling airport, grabbed his bags, and burst out of the door to summon a cab to take him to the university which was only ten miles away. He had just returned from visiting his parents in Tucson, and was now eager to resume training for the track meet.

Just as he stepped to the curb, a cab magically pulled up and the back door swung open. Tommy pitched his bags in, and gratefully slid in, closing the door wearily.

"Where to?"

"The University."

Driving south of the city, the cabbie followed the speed limit until he missed the exit clearly marked University.

"Turn around, man, damn, you just missed my exit. Fuck."

Barely a second had passed when a dark-colored van with large, severely tinted windows approached. Two men hurriedly jumped out, snatched open the back door of the cab, and yanked Tommy out. Forcing him into the van, the driver of the cab came around to take the wheel of the van.

After a few minutes, one of the men spoke. "Tell us about Jamal Morris?"

"He's on the track team same as me."

"What else?"

"There is nothing else."

"Where did he go?"

"He didn't tell me. I don't know."

"Then who might know?"

"Ask Venus."

"Venus?"

"The chick he goes with."

SOULFIRE BOOKS

The three men silently crept up the fire escape. The young fellow they were searching for lived on the fourth floor. His room was situated on the right front quadrant at the top of the grated landing. The men spread out as best they could, standing motionless in the dark until it was unmistakably clear the young man they sought was indeed inside the dorm room. Thus assured, they crashed through the window, shattering the glass into a thousand fragments.

Billy Dudson didn't have a chance to do anything other than to shriek wildly. "Who are you!?"

"Where's Jamal Morris?! Answer me!"

"Who are you talking about?"

One of the masked intruders put the gun under Dudson's chin. "If you don't know where Jamal Morris is, give us the name of someone who does?"

"Venus," the man blurted. "Ask Venus."

Then the men left, but Dudson, like the others, met his Maker.

SOULFIRE BOOKS

"That's interesting." Gentry had just learned that all the members of the track team had unanimously pointed a finger at the same person. "That's very interesting." He coughed into his elbow. "Where's this mystery girl?"

"She's gone too."

"Now, that's highly intriguing," Gentry mused. He looked searchingly at Savoy Brown. "What else can you add to that?"

"Her real name is Venus Staten. Records indicate that she checked into a hotel under that name. The hotel clerk did happen to remember that she was in the company of a young, black male."

"More?"

"The next day she notified the university that she wished to withdraw from her classes."

"What reasons did she give?"

"She was leaving the country."

"Cool," Gentry announced somberly. That's what he always said just when things were starting to heat up.

SIX

Congressman Peterson's office was in disarray

"They're after both of you."

"Who?" Jamal blurted.

"The same men who attacked and killed practically all your buddies on the track team, that's who."

"*What!?*"

"Yep, I just found out. Wiped almost all of them out. Probably figured you may have said something to one of them."

"I didn't, though."

"And they probably know that by now, but what they did manage to get out of them was---."

"Oh my God!" Venus cried, pointing at herself.

"I'm sorry, sweetheart."

"Me, too," Jamal added.

Peterson sighed. "However much anything may be regretted, it's too late for tears. Venus' life is at risk the same as yours."

"Mom? Dad?"

"They're safe."

"Do they know?" Venus asked.

Peterson shook his head. "It took everything in me not to call Kat, and to tell her and Phil to go away, but these people are professionals. The at-random killing is probably over. Most pros are impatient with killing simply for the sake of killing which means your parents will be safe as long as you keep distance between you and them."

Venus sighed in relief.

"Anyway, it's best that I put both of you up for a while. My friend has a place in the country where you'll be safe until someone can make heads or tails out of what could happen next. You must leave right away. I have to stay to finish up a few things, but I'll join you shortly." He looked at Jamal. "I expect to see everything you have, my boy. You have my niece in the middle of this shit, not to mention my sister, so I'm just as serious as the other guys. I'm not taking any bullshit, you hear?"

"Yes sir."

"I have to know so we can fight back. Once I study everything, I'll have a better grasp of what needs to be done. Plus, I have a friend in New York who's an expert on historical documents.

He'll be able to offer some valuable advice and insight on so much we'll need to know. Yeah," Peterson confessed, more to himself than to Venus or Jamal. "Professor Levy will know a thing or two about all of this."

SOULFIRE BOOKS

<<<<<<<<<<<<<<<<<

A day or so later.
Gentry expertly juggled the ham and cheese sandwich
h in one hand while carefully manipulating the mouse with the other, and between bites, he studiously viewed the computer screen, eyeing the latest computerized enhancement of Jamal Morris' school photograph. This one he didn't like so he digitally removed the facial hair, but leaving the mustache, thickened it. Still not satisfied, he reduced the nose, and changed the eye color to a lighter shade of brown. That was more like it.

Over the last two hours, he had graphically experimented with the countless ways the Morris kid might try to disguise himself, and barring major plastic surgery, Gentry felt comfortable that he had programmed them all into his computer database. Now, he would focus on the girl, but first he had some errands to run.

Around 9:00 pm when he again took his seat at his work station, he temporarily suspended all emotion and judgment, suffusing himself with a cold aura of detachment. The girl was exquisite, he noted with solemn aloofness, but he could tell from the twinkle in her eyes that she was still much too young to understand the demonic power of her outrageous beauty, and simply put, would perhaps never attain that knowledge because as of right now, her days were numbered.

Examining her face, he saw no flaws, no tiny imperfections that he could use as a warning signal to make her recognizable to him no matter how fraudulently she disguised herself, but there was nothing. Not even a mole, a freckle, a blemish. Then maybe he would use her perfection as her weakness because no matter what she did cosmetically, she would never be able to mask it.

Voila!

SEVEN

Professor Levy realized he could not let a word of what he was hearing escape his attention for one single second. All of a sudden, he was touched by the likelihood that his future would depend on it, and though he was keenly interested in what his friend, Congressman Peterson, was telling him, he maintained a stoic demeanor. Clearly, he could put a price on this if he could, first of all, put his one and ones together.

When it came time for him to talk, the Professor spoke warmly. "When you are born in this country, your birth certificate is registered and presented to the government as an instrument of commerce, and under the law of commerce, the holder of the birth certificate owns all the legal rights of that individual."

"But ownership denotes slavery, Professor, and that was done away with by the 13th Amendment as you very well know."

"Good observation, Will, but they skirt that violation by not professing ownership of the human, but ownership of the 'Res'. That's Latin which means all the rights of the person named in the birth certificate. It's a fact that our birth certificates were used as collateral for the national debt."

"So whomever holds the birth certificate owns the rights to everything that person owns." A puzzled look crossed Peterson's face. "But the law----."

"The only law that meant anything was called the Uniform Commercial Code, and the UCC is nothing more than a law by bankers."

"But how did that affect the rest of us who were not bankers?"

"Actually, the UCC is commercial contract law and to be subject to it, we must be under contract in one way or another."

"How?"

"Simply by one of the many licenses you own whether it's a driver's license, a marriage license, or a social security number. All or any of these place you under contract to the UCC. You may not know a thing about what going on, but it's all nonetheless binding."

"Come on, Professor," Peterson taunted good-naturedly, "a license?"

"In time, the license became a taxing instrument. For every license, there is a fee which is a tax. In this country, all taxes levied are subject to the UCC due to the nation's bankruptcy. That was the reason Roosevelt nationalized all land in 1933---property taxes. It's all a smokescreen to bilk the people, a clever way to enhance revenues to pay off the bankruptcy. Any time you are hauled into traffic court, say for something like speeding or some other traffic violation, you have violated a civil statute, but yet the fine is a criminal punishment. Shouldn't it be clear that you can't break a civil law and be subject to a criminal penalty?"

By three o'clock in the afternoon, Levy was warmed inside. He felt he had sheltered his self-interest well enough to seem no more than a second-hand observer when his concern ran so much deeper. By now, he no longer entertained the fact that the similarities between Gulliver's and Peterson's requests were warped delusions. No sir, this was the big business of two men trying to make sense out of 1933, and somehow he had fallen smack-dab in the middle of this deadly push-and-pull.

"And another thing is that black people don't have rights, Will. The 14th Amendment only conferred privileges upon them, and privileges will not permit you to pursue legal claims because to have legal standing in a court of law, you must have rights. Your rights as an American, my friend, are a legal fiction set up by the 14th Amendment." The Professor rested his hands in his lap daintily and his face was painted with a pained expression. "I've been able to surmise far more than you have reason to suspect, so I think your very next question should be how to stay alive, Will."

"Huh, what do you mean. I---."

Levy's face was now bright with a sinister glow. "I think the answer to that is obvious so let's not mistake each other or worse yet attempt to mislead each other. We'd both be crazy to play such a foolish game."

"Just what are you saying, Professor?" Peterson's voice had appreciably turned darker. "Please don't waste my time."

Levy stood up. "You do want to live, don't you, Will?"

"I don't like the way this conversation is going." Peterson slowly stood also. "Plus, you have already answered most of the questions---."

"Paul Madsen, dammit. Do I have to drum it into your head that I know what this is all about?"   When Levy saw the congressman's shoulders sag in frustration, he pressed the attack. "I'm too educated not to make the connection, for crying out loud, Will. 1933, the questions about the birth certificates, the other shit you wanted to know. It was a dead giveaway."

Peterson looked tired. "Everything is screwed up, Ace, This could turn out to be a real fiasco."

"Not if you tell me.......everything."

Levy knew he had scored big. Just listening to Peterson made him giddy with excitement, but he also surmised that Gulliver knew about these 'Columbus Day Documents'. But just how much did he know? Probably not the actual identity of the actual people who actually possessed a copy of Paul Madsen's actual document. Hell, he didn't even know since Peterson would be careful to conceal this vital info. Levy had to suppress another smile. Though Peterson might try his damnedest to keep info from him, he'd find out. Already, he'd guessed that it was one of Peterson's constituents from back home, so Levy made a mental note to prepare a list of everyone from Petersons' home district, and once he had checked their personal records, he would have a better grasp of the situation.

"You could have spoken with openness earlier," Levy assured Peterson. "I give you full authority to always level with me. I'm a friend. I'm on your side." Levy smiled. He wasn't taking up a cause, either Peterson's or Gulliver's. He was in this for himself, and would cast his lot on whichever side offered the most incentives. My God, this was going to be fun.

SOULFIRE BOOKS

Gentry slammed the newspaper down on the desk so hard the angry thud echoed across the room with the intense report of a small weapon being discharged. Deftly, he pushed his chair back and stood shakily, taking two steps backwards. He was unhappy.

It was now nearly mid-morning, a beautiful April day in the making, and already he was miserable.

At precisely the bottom of the hour, he picked up the phone in his den and quickly punched in the digits. After a single courtesy ring, the phone was immediately answered.

"Is this you?" Gentry gruffly inquired.

"Yeah," Savoy Brown replied.

"What's up?"

"Apparently, the girl is with the Morris family. She fell off the face of the earth the same day the rest of them did."

"Any chance---."

"Of what, them being right under our noses? No."

"But whole families just don't disappear into thin air."

"Evidently, the Morris family didn't get that memo. Anyway, a whole lot of information wasn't generated about them, but they were a close-knit bunch, kept mostly to themselves. Otherwise, they were just normal people. They just made it a habit not to leave a paper trail of any sort."

"Then you think this was pre-planned?"

"Hell yeah. You just don't go POOF like that without it being tightly organized. Took a lot of finances---."

"And connections."

Brown sighed. "The girl was a little different, though, easier to build, but it was just a freak coincidence that she ended up with the family."

"A lot of good that does me," Gentry cracked. "It's hardly likely than anyone in her family knows shit about anything, The taps on the phone have proved that. Shit, her family is in the blind just the same as everyone else."

"I agree, but for the record, the girl has an uncle who is a congressman."

"Who!?" Gentry blurted uncontrollably. *"Who?!"*

"Peterson. Wilfred Peterson."

Gentry turned the name over and over in his head, trying to associate a face with the name. "That doesn't strike a chord. Wilfred Peterson. Is he new in Washington?"

Brown chuckled. "He's an old coon, been around Capitol Hill for years. Member of the CBC, real workhorse."

"You figure---."

"Don't know and won't say, but if push came to shove, he might be the one she would contact to get her out of this."

"Instinct tells me that you just might be right on that score, so put a collar on him, and see if we can't make some dominoes fall."

"Sounds logical to me," Brown whispered before hanging up. He had always liked the way dominoes fell when you tipped them over, one right after another.

EIGHT

"Have you ever been to Mississippi before?" Venus asked.
"No," Jamal replied distastefully. "Mississippi?"
"You'll like it once you get used to it. It's down home."
"Too down home, if you ask me."
Venus giggled. "Well, at least, you'll like Uncle Frank."
At seven o'clock, Jamal and Venus arrived in Mississippi.

<<<<<<<<<<<<<<<<<
SOULFIRE BOOKS
<<<<<<<<<<<<<<<<<

Professor Levy felt the information was so irrefutable that he took an extended leave of absence from the University, and had high-tailed it, without delay, to Mississippi. In all the world, there appeared to be no better place to concentrate his search for the owners of the 'Columbus Day' documents.

Despite Congressman Peterson leaving the source unnamed, it was overwhelmingly clear that the individual or individuals were his constituents, and the scores of recent phone calls back and forth between him and Bolivar County practically guaranteed it. Something was shaking in Ole Miss.

Levy mourned his desperation, but jumped to life when the phone in the small, cramped office rang. He crossed his fingers as the second man in the room, answered the call. The conversation was brief.

"What was that about?' Levy inquired as soon as Stacey Alexander had hung up the phone.

"You're a pretty smart cookie, Professor."

"At a time like this," Levy cracked, "compliments are ridiculous. Did our odds improve with that phone call?"

"It never occurred to me until a second ago that you knew what you were talking about, but according to my sources----."

"That phone call?" Levy said abruptly.

"That was Grohl, a technical expert when it comes to tracking movement, and for one reason or another, there has been a lot of movement in Bolivar County lately."

Levy's eyes grew wide. "Really?"

Grohl can study transportation info from airlines, trains, and buses. He can also look at local data concerning hotel reservations or bookings, and can tell if people are coming or going. If there's a pattern either way, that buzzard will sniff it out."

"Fascinating."

"And what else is strange at the moment is that there have already been two separate groups of newcomers arriving in town. And guess what else?"

"Humor me."

"That buddy of yours, the Congressman. Well, his number is all over the landscape."

"Fascinating," Levy mused. "I see."

"It's my guess that he's quarterbacking something, and it has to be big from all the calls he's made. Whatever it is he's got going on, I just hope there's enough of it go around because if it's not, bullets are going to start flying."

Levy dealt with something solely in his head before he responded. "You could be wrong about the violence."

"Not hardly, and from what you've told me, when the prize is that big, everyone in the hunt is bullet-prone. Trust me."

Again Levy thought something over before a reply. "Before you take any violent action, clear it with me first."

The derisive laughter was instant. "Then you must not be in any hurry to get this over with. This is not like giving an essay test, Professor, where you politely ask all the little girls and boys to keep their books closed. This is different. Out here in the real world, death is not a passing grade."

Levy raised his eyebrows quizzically.

"The longer you sit around congratulating yourself on your high IQ," Alexander said, "the easier it will be for the other guys to rack up points. I say we move quickly. Let me hire a couple of goons because if this score is what you say it is, I don't want to end up with the short end of the stick."

The Professor dropped his head in his hands, gently massaging his temples. "I don't particularly care to kill."

"Might not can be helped because the closer it gets to October, everybody from the President on down is going to join the hunt, and no one is going to be willing to cooperate with anyone else." The detective sighed. "This is winner take all."

"Yeah, yeah, I imagine you're right," Levy lamented, "but that doesn't necessarily mean that I'm giving you permission to start a gun-fight."

"Just let me handle this my way, and I guarantee to get the job done." Alexander turned completely towards Levy. "Tell me again about how you're going to make me Secretary of Defense?"

SOULFIRE BOOKS

Three days later. Thursday night. Mississippi.

The young, black man yelled hysterically when one of the cops lunged at him, knocking him off his feet, but with a strength the cop didn't expect, the youth flung the officer off him, and as quick as a flash, had grabbed the service revolver from the holster.

"Back up!" the youth screamed, pointing the gun at the officer that was still armed. "Drop your gun!" He looked from one cop the other. I don't wanna kill you."

"Take it easy," the cop on the ground pleaded. "Don't do something you'll end up regretting."

"Shut up," the boy yelled. "I'm not bullshitting. I'm not asking you again to drop your gun, man,"

"Relax, "I'm reaching for my belt," the officer whispered, "so don't shoot. Look, so you can see what I'm doing, so you'll know I'm not trying anything funny. Look."

It was too late when the young kid caught the movement out of the corner of his eye, and before he could react, the officer on the ground had yanked a small caliber weapon from inside his boot, and began firing wildly. The bullets struck the black boy everywhere, but it was the 'lucky shot' between the eyes that killed him.

"Are you okay?" the cop with the gun asked his partner.

The other cop, dazed, nodded mutely. "Yeah."

"Is-is he dead, you think?"

"Hell yeah, he's dead. Now, let's get out of here."

"Better him than us, right?'

<<<<<<<<<<<<<<<<
SOULFIRE BOOKS
<<<<<<<<<<<<<<<<<

Same night. Forty minutes later.

The Mississippi streets glistened with the shiny, wet slickness left over from the rain of over an hour ago, and though it was dark on the wide avenue, the men in the unmarked police car could clearly see the young, black man in the vehicle ahead. Parked a few yards behind the late model SUV, the unmarked car pulled out when the SUV did, and following not-too-closely circled the block. *No one paid attention to the blue sedan.*

At the light, Jamal steered right, and headed back towards the highway. Staring dismally at the white lines, he picked up the phone. "Be there in a minute," he told Venus. Afterwards, he pressed the button to disconnect the call, and as soon as the line was free, he dialed a second number. "I don't like it down here," he sadly whispered. "I'm ready to move on, go some place else." Jamal tapped his fingers on the steering wheel impatiently.

"Where are you? I hear traffic."

"Out for a short drive. Had to get---."

"Fully alert now, Congressman Peterson snapped. "I thought I told you not to be out?"

"Yeah, well, what's a drive around the block?"

"Listen, Jamal," Peterson rasped gruffly, "and listen to me damn good. Go to the house and stay there."

The phone clicked dead.

Jerry Flood, a red-neck, local cop, stared silently at the back of the SUV and reached under the dash for the siren. He confronted his partner. "May I suggest we get this over with?"

"Do you hear me arguing?"

Officer Flood rolled down the window on the passenger side and slammed the siren atop. "Lights, camera, action," he exclaimed happily.

With an anguished whoop, the siren howled ON, flashing garishly in the darkened gloom, lighting up the swollen blackness like a wounded, metallic firefly.

"Shit!" Jamal groaned. "Cops." Then he relaxed and slowed down. He hadn't done anything wrong. Turning on his hazard lights, he pulled over and parked, waiting on the cops.

A short time later, Jamal found himself pressed violently over the hood of the unmarked car, his body twisted at a grotesque angle, his arms throbbing where the cuffs had been put on too tightly behind his back.

"Oww!" Jamal screamed loudly, "I haven't done anything."

"Yeah, yeah," one of the cops growled, "that's what they all say. Now, shut up."

"I don't understand," Jamal yelped. "Let me go."

"Show him what we think of that," Flood declared, lighting up a cigarette.

"For being such an asshole, we gotta tighten your cuffs a teeny bit. How's this?" Officer White snarled, squeezing the cuffs until Jamal screamed wildly. "Feels good, huh?"

Flood laughed. "Make him make that sound again."

"What? This sound." White squeezed the cuffs brutally.

"Owww!"

"Yeah, that's the one. A nigger screaming is like music to my ears." Flood grinned at his partner. "Wanna hear the chorus?" He bared his teeth. "Listen to this." He sucked on the cigarette until the tip glowed red-hot, then blew noisily, scattering the ashes. He pointed the flaming Marlboro at Jamal's exposed neck. "Watch, listen, and learn."

Abruptly the cops turned, their attention focused on the shadows. Flood gasped, dropping the cigarette. Officer White's hands flew lightning quick to his service revolver. Panic-stricken, he yanked at his weapon, knowing instinctively that he was much too late. Flood had already calculated the chances of a successful draw, and knew they were about as good as winning the lottery so, all of sudden, became visibly religious. He made the sign of the cross and begged the Lord for forgiveness. A second later, shots rang out, renting the night with a quick series of muffled thumps.

Jamal flipped over in time to see one of the cop's heads arch back, then snap like a whip as the second bullet penetrated his skull. Jamal closed his eyes, not seeing what happened exactly to the cop's partner, but he clearly heard the gun's muffled discharge. Oh my God! Was he next?

Suddenly, Jamal felt himself being yanked forward violently. "Let's go, dammit!" The man half-pushed, half-dragged Jamal to the dark blue sedan, "Get it!" He shoved Jamal into the driver's seat.

"Wh-what's happening?"

"Shut up and let me get these fucking handcuffs off." The black man attempted to insert the key. "Be still, nigga. We ain't got all damn night to do this shit." Wrestling briefly with the cuffs, the man finally freed Jamal's hands. "Now, drive us the hell out of here."

"Where?" Jamal massaged his aching wrists.

"I'll give you instructions," the man snarled. "You just go where I tell you to go."

Driving quickly away from the dead bodies, Jamal could sense the strange man's piercing gaze, and a new sense of panic erupted from deep within his bowels. He despaired, then mentally upbraided himself for letting his imagination run away with him as he forestalled his apprehensions by confronting himself with the untested knowledge that the man was not, by any account, one of the 'mysterious men'. Invoking the mercy of God, he tried to sound tough. "What's up, man? Why you waste those devils back there?"

"You think they gave a fuck about you, nigga? If I hadn't rescued your ass, they would have killed you just as quick as I killed them."

"But they were cops."

"How many black men have been saved because of that fact?"

Out of the corner of his eye, Jamal had no problem seeing the gun cradled in the man's lap, his finger looped casually around the trigger. Jamal knew better than to offer a challenge, but he had to request some information. "I hate to sound ungrateful for what you did for me, but what I need to know is why. I mean, I--."

"The man's cell phone rang, interrupting Jamal. The man raised the gun, pointing it at Jamal all the while activating the audible on the speaker so the call would come through aloud.

"Yo."

"Brown?" The voice filled the car with an ominous menace. "What's happening?"

"There were problems."

"Major."

"They're minor, now."

The sigh of relief uttered by the man on the other end of the line was so palpable it felt like the air going out of one of the tires. The hissing filled the car. "And the subject?"

Brown stared at Jamal, smiling. "Say hello to Mister Gentry, Jamal."

At once, Jamal knew how unsafe he presently was.

"Where are you now?" Gentry asked.

"On the road."

"You bringing him in?"

"Hell no. Fuck you."

"You black jungle bunny. What, you double-crossing me. Is that it, you bastard?"

"Will you ever forgive me?" Brown taunted in a mimicking tone. "Goodbye you cheating ass, white motherfucker."

"Hey wait, let's negotiate. Please don't---."

Just as Brown arched forward to depress the button, Jamal moved in the same exact instant. He stomped down on the brake pedal with a powerful heave of his foot, and just as the terribly unexpected motion jerked Brown forward, Jamal's right arm lashed out, gripping the man's pistol hand while he simultaneously twisted his body half-way around, enabling him to smash the heel of his palm into the bridge of Brown's nose, smashing cartilage and bone. Unfazed by his abrupt violence, Jamal smashed his fist into Brown's face a second time, shoving what was left of the man's nose practically down his throat.

Brown slumped forward, gurgling wetly as blood streamed down his face. Frantically, Jamal reached over, and opening the passenger door, pushed Brown out of the car before speeding off. Breathing raggedly, he tried desperately to give a full account of what had just happened, and what to do next. Unsanctified paranoia played with his mind, but he was coherent enough to know he couldn't return to get Venus. He snatched up the phone. "Venus!" he screamed, "that house is not safe. Get out!"

"Jamal, wh---."

"They're here, Venus. The mysterious men. I-I've seen them. Run, Venus!"

<<<<<<<<<<<<<<<<
SOULFIRE BOOKS
<<<<<<<<<<<<<<<<

Over the years, many of his adversaries had recalled that Gentry, once angered, was like something out of this world. Some said, he was like the devil while others, remarkably enough, had likened him to a death angel.

Angel or devil notwithstanding, Gentry was mad, was as riled up as a nest of hornets, and that was precisely the reason why, when he kicked the door in at the house where he knew the girl was, he was not in the mood to be fucked with.

"Let's not bullshit, bitch," he yelled, a gun in each hand, "come out with your fucking hands up."

He was so angry, he fired a perfect shot into one of the table lamps, striking it dead-center, sending bits of glass flying every which way. He fired another shot into the wall, hoping the mere act of discharging his weapon would reduce the wired-up fire inside his brain. It didn't. Still, he fired another time.

Hearing noise, he raced to the window as Venus scrambled out of the back door.

"Dammit, you black whore! Come back here!"

<<<<<<<<<<<<<<<<
SOULFIRE BOOKS
<<<<<<<<<<<<<<<<

Exactly one hour later.

Venus could hardly breathe. She had no sense of time, and the gag in her mouth had a bitter, oily taste. Her blood pressure had skyrocketed, and every part of her body felt wounded, more dead than alive.

"You have just begun to feel my wrath," Gentry snarled with an evil grin. "Before I get finished with you, I'll make you pray for death."

Venus knew perfectly well that the man meant what he said. His vicious attack upon her had been brutal and merciless, interrupted only by her falling unconscious.

Gentry slapped Venus across the mouth with the back of his hand. "Do we have an understanding, black whore?"

Venus didn't have any choice but to nod her head weakly. She dared not anger the man any further.

Gentry slapped Venus again. "I don't take kindly to people, niggers especially, who make me work harder than I want to. First, that nappy-headed boyfriend of yours, then my no-account help." He glared at Venus. "Good help is so hard to find these days. And then I had to go chasing you down like I'm some goddamn track star." He slapped Venus once more.

When she regained consciousness, Venus found that the ringing din in her ears would not stop, but that was quite understandable given how hard she had been hit. If he would just ask for info, she would willingly provide it, so there was absolutely no cause for the man to torture her.

Gentry leaned down until he was damned near nose to nose with the sorely battered face of the young, black woman. "It would be insulting to me, if, at this moment, you have devised, in your mind, little childish games to play with me. I caution you not to try. I will kill you. Now, what I expect of you, starting right now, are answers. Nothing less will be tolerated. Any play on words, any double-talk, any nonsense at all will bring you to a horrible end. Do I make myself clear, young lady?" He pulled himself upright, his voice patiently and fatherly. "Tell me about your boyfriend?" The gag was roughly yanked away. "It is not your duty to evaluate what I ask you. Just respond, okay? Your boyfriend, I want you to acquaint me with him."

Between abnormal gasps for air, Venus parroted personal data, watching warily as Gentry sucked up her words like a sponge.

"Any word on his mother's parents?"

"No." The answer was honest enough. "I only met her once, and she was upset that Jamal had told me about their family secret."

That squared with Gentry. He nodded. "That night, the night you were with the family, where were you?"

"A house. I'm not sure where. There was too much to think about and I was afraid. Plus Jamal was driving crazy, going every which way to get there, but then suddenly we were there."

"I see. How did they make the house explode?"

Venus shrugged. "I don't know. They may--."

"Then don't bother trying to explain. Speculation will simply annoy me, and you know what that will bring, don't you?"

Venus began to cry. "Please, you have hurt me enough, and I've told you everything except where the secret documents are, and there are in a safe at my Uncle Willie's house, and if you let me go, I'll give you the address and the combination to the safe. Please."

SOULFIRE BOOKS

A few days later.

"That's just what I thought, Gentry laughed to himself when he observed the Washington, DC residence of Congressman Wilfred Peterson . "A piece of cake."

Standing not far from the front entrance, it suddenly hit him like a ton of bricks that soon he would possess Madsen's bastard papers, and this so pleased him that he found it difficult not to express his euphoria with a song and dance. "Good thinking," he told himself as he nixed the idea. Still, he felt genuinely ecstatic since getting in would prove to be nothing more than a practice run. He congratulated the Congressman for being so security-foolish. By the time Gentry reached the front door, he had his emotions fully under control. He had a job to do. Afterwards, he'd take the rest of the day off to celebrate, get drunk. Lay a broad. Whatever.

Since he knew where everything was inside the house, he felt relieved of any time constraints. This would be a quick in and out job. Happily, he stared at the lock on the door, and had no complaint. It was a poor, distant relative of the newer, more indefensible models of today, so it wasn't but a second before the door slung open.

Inside, Gentry was excited but also hell-bent on being professional. He weaved through the spacious home, dripping silent footsteps across the plush carpet, but in the study, he went immediately to the safe, which was exactly where the bitch had said it would be. May God bless her soul, Gentry snickered as his right hand went for the grooved, oval knob on the safe's combination lock. Then it felt as though he was on fire.

Next came darkness.

SOULFIRE BOOKS

Congressman Peterson spit on the dead, white man in the den. An eye for an eye. The bastard had murdered his niece, but Venus knew the bastard would, at least, get his also, She had been instructed, if the situation were to arise, to use the ruse about the papers being in his safe, but what she wouldn't tell him was that the safe was electrified. The cast iron vault had fried the man alive.

"Get his dead, white ass out of here," Peterson instructed Khalil Cinque, his most trusted friend. He suddenly didn't care what they did with the body. He merely wanted it removed from the rental house so that he could get the place cleaned.

Abruptly, without introducing themselves, two more black men rushed into the den, but slowed down when they saw Cinque.

"What did you dig up?"

"Barlow Gentry, that was his name. Specialized in covert operations both inside and outside the military. Heavy-duty dude, just the type you would expect to be in on something like this."

"Pull up everything on him," Cinque commanded. "We need to be able to trace his movements in the hopes of chasing down his employer."

"That dead devil was linked to the Merchant family in New York," the man said. "At least, that's who paid him. The Merchants are rich, filthy rich, own a lot of shit here and overseas."

"Look, man," Peterson sighed, "I'm going to have to take a few days leave. I need to go to stay with Kat until after the funeral."

"Then are you coming back as Willie the politician, or Jomo the conqueror?" Cinque waited.

"Someone killed my niece, my sister's only child. Do I need to say anything else?"

As they walked from the house and converged on their cars, Cinque stopped his friend. "There is something else, my comrade."

"Say it."

Cinque gripped Peterson's shoulder. "The United Black Army wants it in writing that upon the successful conclusion of this mission that we get ceded two separate states of our own." He stared into Peterson's eyes.

"That's not an unreasonable request. You've got it, my brother."

"Power to the people," Cinque uttered fervently." When Peterson simply nodded in response, Cinque pulled the Congressman into a powerful embrace. "This is it, Jomo. After all these years, the struggle is about to bear fruit. The black man will be king again. The Almighty sure does work in mysterious ways, but man, I'm not complaining. This is the yellow-brick road, Jomo. We're home."

Naturally, Congressman Peterson chose not to argue, but he didn't feel like he was on a stairway to heaven. This felt more like a march into hell.

NINE

Nearly forty-five minutes had passed since Jamal had made contact with one of the Congressman's friends, and he still hadn't gotten a call-back. Already, he was antsy which, by the way, made him feel like prey, and there was nothing admirable about feeling like a pig in a sausage factory.

When he finally did get his call-back, it was not the welcoming news he had hoped for. Besides all the black power rhetoric that jingled like slogans from the 60s, all the instruction he received was-----*wait*. Considering his dire predicament, waiting was the most outrageous request anyone could demand of him. Compared to what he had hoped for, waiting was a surprisingly thin choice, but neither was he particularly attracted to the idea of getting killed which could very well be the next big thing if the other guys sniffed him out.

Across the broad terrain of possibilities, Jamal tended to favor any plan that catered to his self-interest: staying alive. Without a doubt, he was for any scheme that complemented his ability to continue sucking down gobs and goo-gobs of sparkling, fresh oxygen.

The phone rang.

"Stay put," the caller instructed, "we're on the way."

Before hanging up, the man managed to cite a few more 60ish slogan that, for the life of Jamal, didn't bear one thin dime's worth of relevance to any of the basic political or social realities of the 21st century. And it was deliberately strange to him why Venus' uncle would entrust this mission to a bunch of black guys trapped in a time warp.

Another phone call a few minutes after the ominous '*stay put*' call instructed him to exit the hotel via the delivery entrance, and to sit tight in his car. Someone would be there within minutes.

Ten minutes later, a black Caddy rounded the corner and before Jamal knew it, a man had snatched open his car door and was nudging him over to the passenger side. Another man jumped into the back seat.

"I'm driving," the big, black man said firmly.

"You're with Uncle Willie?"

The man slammed the door and started the engine. "Whaddya think?"

"I don't know," Jamal snapped, "that's why I asked."

The man stared at Jamal blankly. "Don't you think it's a little too late to be concerned about who's who. I've already commandeered your ride, and my partner in the backseat has a gun big enough to knock an elephant to his knees, and now you decide to be cautious." The man laughed. "Didn't even have your damned door locked. That was stupid. You should have known better, and you should have had a piece."

"I have a gun."

"Where is it?'

"In the trunk," Jamal replied sheepishly.

The driver looked Jamal over. "A lot of good it will do you back there. What 'hood you from out of?"

"Don't come down too hard on him, Akeem. He's only a young scrub, still probably believe the white man is Santa Claus."

Jamal pouted angrily. "No offense, but a black racist is no better than a white one."

Both men laughed.

"Nigga, you crazy," the driver announced sadly.

"And let me think," Jamal snapped bitterly, "both of you are African royalty."

"Not exactly," the driver said, "but as members of the Untied Black Army, we are 100% Afro-centric, meaning everything we do evolves from a black perspective."

"I find that unusual since most of what we do in this country has an European origin."

"Tell me, then," the driver snapped rudely, "if you're so white-man smart, why your Caucasian friends want to kill you so badly."

"Like they did your girlfriend."

"W-what did you just say?" Jamal turned to face the man in the backseat.

"Yeah, that's right. The crackers iced your woman, man."

"No!" Jamal shook his head in abject disbelief. "No! This can't be true what you're saying. Can't be Venus.....naw, man."

"It's true. The girl, the Congressman's niece. She's dead."

"And buried,"

Jamal shivered involuntarily. He'd never been good at handling bad news, and though he was not overly religious, he did whisper a prayer for his girlfriend's soul. Now, he felt absolutely nothing. He was numb. Comfortably numb.

<<<<<<<<<<<<<<<<
SOULFIRE BOOKS
<<<<<<<<<<<<<<<<

"And just who the hell do you think you're fooling? If it's not true, then why all the fuss and bother. Come on, Willie, give me some credit. I'm never that grossly mistaken."

Congressman Peterson considered Levy's passionate protest, and immediately realized the professor posed an eminent danger because his greed was all too clear. At first, Levy had presented himself as a friend, but that guise soon wore thin when Peterson raised serious objections about his feelings about meddling in the affairs of black folks.

"Consider how fortunate you are, Will, that it was me that stumbled upon this instead of say, practically anyone else in the world. At least, you can be thankful that I'm not a man of violence, and by the way, I'm awfully sorry about your niece. Please extend my condolences to Katherine."

"You've been an astute observer, haven't you, Professor?"

"Life is a game of chances, and I see only those things that enhance my chances of making better choices. No one, my friend, exists in a vacuum. It's quite the reverse, and good fortune is an amenity that everyone is in search of."

"And yon felt it would be to your advantage to stir up what I'd told you, and to look for amenities." Peterson scowled. "That's a terrible abuse of friendship, Ace. It stinks."

"Yes, I take it that you would see it that way, but do you really think we have time to debate? I don't think we can afford it."

Peterson was still fuming. "It just galls me how you---."

"What, found out?' Blame yourself for not being more careful. I simply played a good hunch. When you disclosed the little you did, I already had enough prior information to know what was cooking, and I knew all roads led to Mississippi."

"So without concern for---/"

"And after I read the newspaper about Venus," Levy interrupted, "everything was confirmed. The rest of the pieces fell together in no particular order, but with a good enough fit that I could come to you and lay my cards out on the table. What should matter now, Will, is that I know who the other guys are, and I could just as well have gone to them. I'm quite sure they wouldn't be sitting across from me, staring at me like I was a wolf in sheep's clothing. Instead, the bastards would welcome me with open arms."

Perhaps more quickly than he had anticipated, the Congressman found that he was already carving up the spoils of Paul Madsen's great sweepstakes. A couple of states to the UBA, and in due course, whatever it would take to pacify the Professor, and with genuine interest, the Congressman wondered just what that would be.

"I imagine you want to be President," Peterson joked laughingly.

Levy laughed along, but didn't answer.

TEN

48 hours later. Mississippi.

On the basis of the coroner's report, and all the other evidence that turned up during the investigation, the DA decided to charge Officer Rand with first degree murder in the shooting death of the unarmed black youth.

Within hours of the indictment, every attorney from the Prosecutor's Office was begging for the case, but still suffering from a major loss in their last, big murder case, the Chief Prosecutor was in no hurry to assign anyone the task. He wanted to make a strong case and to leave a lasting impression, but that would require a radically different approach to this case. The Chief Prosecutor pondered his options.

Determined to prevent another judicial debacle from occurring in Bolivar County, Chief Prosecutor Robert Cathcart knew he had to prosecute the case himself, and after embracing this prospective, nurtured the initial X's and O's of his trial strategy, but for some reason, he felt pursued by the haunting belief that this case was going to be so big, it was going to change the course of human history.

Cathcart laughed aloud in his empty office. "Imagine that," he   said.

SOULFIRE BOOKS

72 hours later. New York.

At first, East didn't get it. *Then he did.* Bolting upright in bed when he saw the late night news about the police in Mississippi charged with the murder of the young, black man, he snatched up the phone, dialing Gulliver.

"Turn on the news," he said.

"That shit is not news, cops killing niggers. Have you lost your fucking mind, East?"

"This is it. This is what you wanted."

"It is? What the fuck are you talking about?"

"I'm taking that case. I'm going to defend that cop, and you are going to pay me for doing it."

"East, you're bonkers. The kid was unarmed."

"Fuck that. It's not about the nigger," East bragged. "It's about the nigger not having any rights, civil or otherwise, that the cop had to deal with."

"How?"

"The 14th Amendment, my boy. This is it. I'm going to win the case by stripping away the so-called authority of the 14th Amendment. It's sorta like a test case. I win this, and prove the nigga kid had no legal standing, come October----."

"Dammit, East, I love you. Go bring me back the 14th Amendment on a fucking silver platter."

"No problem, Boss," East laughed. "I'm going to blow that country prosecutor out of the water. This case has just gotten too damn big for him."

BOOK THREE

ONE

Jamal looked from one man to the other, and found nothing entertaining in either of their black faces. Uneasily, he shifted his focus to Congressman Peterson.

"Our position is deteriorating," Peterson confessed, "and that's about the long and the short of it." To the left and partially hidden by the thick drapes, a strikingly beautiful, middle-aged woman signaled to the congressman, who instantly stood, without excusing himself, and followed her down the hallway.

"After all these years," Cinque remarked bitterly, "I'm ready to shoot it out. Ever since I was a child, I've had to take shit off the white oppressor. As in Claude McKay's poem, let us die gloriously."

When Peterson returned to the room, he commented slowly. "Certainly, everyone knows that wasn't good news." His voice was far from warm and inviting. "But at least, it wasn't the end of the world bad news I was expecting."

Cinque studied his friend who sat across from him. "Let's go out fighting, Jomo. You, of all people, should know that you can't make a deal with the devil."

Peterson ignored the retort. "Now, to the latest news." Peterson wet his lips with his tongue. "Professor Levy called---."

"Man," Cinque blurted, "I trust that cracker like a mongoose trusts a snake."

Peterson closed his eyes tightly. "I think---."

"I'll tell you what I think," Cinque interrupted. "I think that no-good cracker is going to sell us out. I'm not joking, Jomo. Selling a nigga out is what crackers do. We're going to get bamboozled, Jomo. I've got a sixth sense about shit like this, and I say the double-cross already done came and gone."

After a few more seconds, Peterson firmly broke off Cinque's rant by declaring that a decision had been made, and that everyone must prepare to obey the instructions.

Angry, Cinque sighed in resignation. *"Damn!"*

"Professor Levy informs us that the Merchant family wants to settle this without a resort to bloodshed." Peterson paused, measuring what he would say next. "What he proposes in unusual to say the least, but our chances are just as good as theirs."

"Said the cat to the rat."

Akeem agreed with Cinque. "Sounds like famous last words."

"Just what is this unusual deal?" Jamal asked quietly.

"Instead of killing, it is suggested that we battle....in court."

"In court?!" Cinque shouted loudly. "What do they take us for, idiots? He pointed an accusing finger at the Congressman. "Do you actually believe those devils are going to let us waltz into a courtroom anywhere in this country, presenting a claim as outlandish as ours, and then let us just walk out of the building with the damn deed to the country in our back pocket. Come on, man, what kind of sense does that make? It's a bigger bushwhack than what Custer got at Little Big Horn, And I can't believe you'd even invest thought on that bullshit."

Peterson held up his hand to throttle his friend. "Until we invent something better or more satisfying, this is it."

Cinque groaned pitifully. "Ahh, man."

The Congressman's mood turned decidedly more edgy, then melted into a stoic professionalism. "In my home district, a murder case is scheduled to take place. A white cop killed an unarmed, black kid."

"Pardon me, brotha," Cinque announced softly, "but what does that have to do with our situation?"

"Everything."

"How's that?" Even Jamal was skeptical.

"Be patient. Let me explain."

To lie would have offered a tempting shortcut, but Congressman Peterson didn't want anyone to be surprised by what was to come. Deception was an element he felt had no validity in a crisis with a reputation as big as this one. The most he would allow himself was that---here and there---he might trim the facts to reduce the shock potential, but basically he'd give it to them as it had been originally given to him. For a second, he wondered what his voice would sound like. He wanted to sound cool, yet detached; vibrant without any hint of dryness, and most surely he hoped to shun boring repetition, but no matter how spare the language or how poetic, the bottom line was the exact same: all of black America would die unless they stayed in their place.

But what really concerned the Congressman was that the Merchant family was extremely unapologetic about what would occur, and had displayed no reluctance in detailing how horrific the event would be, if, by chance, he made any abrupt break from the scripted program. And it was his duty, he had been told, to deter anyone else's foolishness. The Merchant family had been so straightforward, they had let it be known that they would not even tolerate any verbal challenge. The family also made sure it was clear to Peterson just how committed they would be to carrying out any threat they made, and Peterson had no reason not to believe that the military, upon command, would be ready to move in.

"To give you a measure of our vulnerability," Peterson spoke directly to Cinque, "while unbeknownst to the rest of the world, as of this moment, The King Alfred Plan--."

"Dammit, Jomo," Cinque exclaimed. "Naw, man, not that. We're sitting ducks."

"W-what is this King Alfred Plan?" Jamal asked.

"Some shit that they don't teach niggas in them bullshit schools where you go to get educated, but FYI, the King Alfred Plan is a military strategy where US troops overrun the ghettoes, wiping us out." Cinque sulked. "Bullshit-assed motherfuckers."

"The Plan was put into effect," Akeem continued, "back in the days before any of us were born because the whiteys felt that one day blacks might revolt., so when they stuffed niggas in the ghetto, they had a reason for concentrating them in one place. We would be easier to get to."

Jamal looked at the Congressman for confirmation.

"That's right," Peterson added. "That's why they developed low-income projects so close to major highways. This way they could move the tanks in quickly and quell---."

"Dammit, Jomo," Cinque barked, "now, we have no choice but to fight. Let's make history."

Peterson grunted loudly. "And what will that history say? That we were crazy-assed fools. I admire your courage, Cinque, but white people will come together as never before if we try to cash in come October. You'll have lil old, white ladies manning tanks, dashing into the hood like General Patton. I'm telling you."

Jamal shuddered. "What do we have to do?"

"Duke it out in court." Peterson shrugged heavily. "It's as simple as that."

"Ain't no more of the OJ shit happening, Jomo."

"Naturally," Peterson said, "that is my sentiment exactly, but this case will not be shaped by traditional law. It's not going to be centered around either the innocence or guilt of anyone in a technical sense."

Jamal stopped the Congressman. "But all trials are about guilt or innocence, even civil ones. I can't imagine anything else being more important in a court of law in this country."

"Well, this is an isolated case where nothing will be what it appears to be to the rest of the world because behind everyone's back, we'll be battling for ownership of the country. Winner take all."

"America is on trial?" Jomo asked, confused.

"It's a grandly designed scheme," Peterson confessed admiringly, "and at first even I didn't get it, but I had to admit that it is a brilliant way to conduct our battle."

"I think you've lost it, brotha" Cinque cracked . "Just what is our position, anyway?"

"We embrace the prosecutor's position."

"I don't get it," Jamal said.

"At the same time the defense is fighting for the cop, they will also be seeking to repeal the 14th Amendment." Peterson could not help but notice the confused look on the men's faces. He smiled. "The cop's lawyer will be arguing that his client is not guilty of murder since the young brotha had no rights, and was not entitled to equal protection under the law. Their claim is that he was stateless, a non-citizen, and therefore had no rights the cop was bound to respect."

"Oh my God," Cinque gasped. "Dred Scott!"

"All over again, my brotha, unless we prevail. Our contention will be that the 14th Amendment awarded citizenship to us."

Akeem nodded, getting the picture. "A secretive, selective war on the 14th Amendment because minus the rights of citizenship, come Columbus Day, our claims won't mean shit, no matter what Paul Madsen said or did."

"Bingo!" said the Congressman.

<<<<<<<<<<<<<<<<<

SOULFIRE BOOKS

<<<<<<<<<<<<<<<<<

All of this was at odds with what Gulliver really wanted to do which was to kill the Morris family and be done with it, but there was a good reason to submit to East's proposal: It just might work. However, the other guys had to accept the cop's murder trial as the pretext for the battle. It was very clever and Gulliver applauded that, but there were detriments, the main one being that the niggers had an equal chance of winning, and that greatly upset him. Damn, it was such a big risk. The built-in tension inside his head continued to swell, giving rise to fears he detested, but had to tolerate. Aware of these stakes, no degree of carelessness would be acceptable. The playing field was too level for that.

"Damn."

Gulliver regarded his upset stomach and the tension headache as the proper reaction to his dilemma. He also learned that no matter what, he could not turn a blind eye to the interests of the other guys. Hell, they wanted to win as badly as he did, and though he didn't, for a minute, believe they could reach his standards financially, they sure as hell wasn't going to let money deter them. No doubt, these niggers were going to throw money at this trial, heaping it on like it was red-eye gravy, and with the current mood, they didn't have shit to lose.

"Damn!"

Gulliver's stomach belched, and a bucket of acid seemed to churn in his intestines. He had better remember that the other guys were not going to put together a 'Simple Simon' piecemeal case, and though he had no clue as to how their case would evolve, he knew it would be a carefully arranged step-by-step campaign to bury white America.

"Just how dicey is this going to get?"

"You'll get through it," East proclaimed arrogantly.

"That's not good enough, dammit." I want the odds calculated down to their naked-assed essence, and I want to know exactly what you're going to do in case there's an emergency." Gulliver took a deep breath. "I'm asking for an estimate right now, and I don't want to hear none of that lawyer bullshit about there not being any guarantees."

East faced Gulliver squarely. "Most of the arguments were done long ago, and now all that remains for me to do is to fit the case with a legal prosthesis and make it walk on water."

"And you can do that."

"A lot better than most," East bragged, "but certain perks are required. "When East saw Gulliver cast a wary glance at him, he grinned. "Don't worry, they're relatively few, and they will be needed to stimulate the morale of my staff."

"What do you want, East?"

"Don't sound so brutal," the lawyer teased. "Given your immense resources, this will be almost painless."

"Spit it out, East, and stop being cute."

"In that case, I demand that you stay out of my business. I'm a professional, highly competent, and don't wish to be harassed and needled over the way I pursue the case." East stared at Gulliver. "When we're in the courtroom, it's my show."

"You're nuts, East, if you think I'm just going to sit on my ass like a fucking knot on a log, and not say shit about the case. *"You're fucking nuts!* I'm standing over you like a buzzard. I'm not about to let no son-of-a-bitch take QuickSilver out for a walk without me being right there to breathe fire down his neck, so no dice there."

"Look---."

"Forget about it, East. No one is going to hog-tie me when the stakes are this high. This point can't be negotiated. I expect to be thoroughly briefed the night before as to what the courtroom strategy will be for the next day and if, for some unknown reason, you decide to switch horses in the middle of the stream, I'm telling you right now to call a goddamn recess so I'll know what's getting ready to go down. Where the empire is concerned, I don't want any surprises."

East didn't argue. "My billing fee is $5000 an hour, plus I expect a more generous bonus at the successful conclusion of this case. Very generous, I must emphasize."

"Go on."

"I want first-class lodging for myself as well as for the other team members, plus a better than modest living wage. We'll need access to quality transportation for local travel, and use of your company jet on weekends so we can be flown home to spend Saturday and Sunday away from our country cousins in Mississippi."

"Anything else, East?'

East thought for a while, "No." he concluded, "but you'll be notified in the event something else arise."

"I'm sure I will."

East pretended not to hear the last remark, and he was not sorry he had set such iron-cast playing rules because he enjoyed seeing Gulliver squirm.

"And the courts will be forced to cooperate once we win this mock trial?"

"It'll hardly be a mock trial. Try that one on police officer Rand, and see how he likes it. I imagine he is shitting bricks even as we speak. He already knows that a Special Prosecutor is being brought in for this case."

"What's with this guy?"

"Who?"

"The Special Prosecutor?"

"Don't know shit about him---yet."

SOULFIRE BOOKS

The first of Maurice Stubbs' ancestors had been captured early, and transported to a slave harbor that faced the Canary Islands. The kidnapped Africans had belonged to the Wolof Kingdom, and were Muslims, but Pope Leo had issued a papal bull declaring that the blacks must be christened before leaving port. As a ceremony, the slaves would be assembled in the main square where a priest would give each of the blacks a Christian name, after which he'd sprinkle salt on their tongues, after which he'd rinse with holy water. Lastly, they would be told to forget their place of birth because they had just been made over.

Since the American colonies had different preferences in regards to the Africans, Stubbs' ancestors ended up in South Carolina. In Charleston, the Wolof were prized because they were good at learning different languages which made it easier for them to grasp the English commands, and on that account, this is where he had been born.

Maurice Stubbs had grown up, wondering just what in the world had his ancestors and the other kidnapped Africans been thinking. Instead of coming to America and boldly demonstrating their industriousness and value as slaves, why hadn't there been an universal 'malingering effect' among them. They should have feigned illness, pretended adverse affects due to the weather, acted as if they didn't understand what was expected of them, worked slow, had fainting spells. Anything but performing as well as they did. If the early slaves would have been wise enough to be as worthless as slaves as the Indians, the slave trade would have grounded to a halt on its own accord, but no, they took to slavery as if they wanted to prove something to the slavemaster. Stubbs had never understood that, but this instinct to act against their own better interest was still alive and well in the black community.

Yet what was he expected to do? It certainly wouldn't be foolish to say no thanks to Congressman Peterson. Until now, no case had ever made him afraid, but this case, this monstrosity had been surely certified by Lucifer himself, and drawn up on the admission parchment from hell. Plus, he saw no true advantage to having this 'hot potato' dropped in his lap.

When the phone rang, Stubbs knew who it was on the other line. He picked up, knowing he was about so say yes to an irreversible situation that, once moving, wouldn't slow down or stop.

"What's the word, brotha?" Congressman Peterson asked.

"Yes."

Nothing more was said.

<<<<<<<<<<<<<<<<
SOULFIRE BOOKS
<<<<<<<<<<<<<<<

New York City.

East's office was quiet, it seemed almost like a morgue, and Gulliver kept wanting to make noise or to do something to liven up the place, but he was tense.

"They'll call," East said reassuringly. "the bait is too irresistible."

"Either this," Gulliver huffed, "or they a
ll die. No bull-shitting."

"Just be patient. My boy, the Congressman, is no fool. If nothing else, his sense of duty will quiet any objections he might have to our proposal." Professsor Levy smiled. "He's a career politician, but he is committed and dedicated, so I don't believe his conscience will allow him to put the entire nigger population under the gun."

"And just what do you know about the law?" East spat.

"I only recognize that most attorneys are trained in the charade of law rather than in its actual practice. At any rate," Levy said matter-of-factly, "they propose a meeting in a rural setting to hammer out certain assurances."

"This is a fucking war, dammit," East wailed loudly, "not the fucking Geneva Convention. I say that once they step their black asses in the courtroom, all is fair."

Gulliver ignored East's outburst and spoke directly to Levy. "Guarantees of what sort?'

"Just certain courtesies so that we won't have to ask the judge to monitor each other's behavior."

"Don't buy that baloney," East chided Gulliver. "Since our resources are far greater than theirs, of course, the bastards will feel inclined to beg for favors. I say, fuck 'em!"

"When?" Gulliver inquired, "and where, exactly."

East groaned audibly.

"Day after tomorrow. Banner Elk, North Carolina."

Gulliver poured himself another drink. "Make the arrangements."

<<<<<<<<<<<<<<<<
SOULFIRE BOOKS
<<<<<<<<<<<<<<<<

North Carolina. The High Country. 9:00am.

For the occasion, the cabin at Old Gwaltney Place on Beech Mountain Parkway had been rented, and the big room with the fireplace had been conveniently arranged to look like a conference hall, but for some reason, the casual ambience of the room had the urban feel of an upscale bohemian speakeasy. That is until the sparks flew.

Gulliver exploded at the sight of the black men. "So, you're the bastards trying to take away what my family has worked all our lives to build," East restrained him. "It won't happen. It won't happen," he spat angrily. "No one will destroy the empire, do you hear me?"

"We're helpless to do anything about the toil you and your family may have put into the building of your so-called empire. I'm not going to cry for you as I'm equally sure none of you cried over slavery, so let's not fool each other." Stubbs exhibited no fear, speaking clearly and forcefully. "Now, if you want to get down to business, we'll let your immature outburst pass."

The room was quite large, but the tension seemed to shrink it considerably. On one side of the table, Levy seated Gulliver and East while the chairs opposite were occupied by Congressman Peterson and Maurice Stubbs, the tall, light-skinned lawyer who bore a striking resemblance to Malcolm X. Levy sat at the head of the table.

Levy swept his eyes over the four men, and felt the hate. Suddenly, he wondered if he could make this work. "What we don't know," he began calmly, "is how this will turn out."

"Bullshit," East rasped spitefully, "it's all over but the shouting."

Neither of the black men responded.

"You know what I think?" Gulliver blurted, "I think you-you blacks finally hope this is your chance to stick it to whitey, but it will never happen. Never. You understand that. Never. All my life, I have had to listen to the black man's agonizing tale about how he's gotten the shaft in this country, so let me explain how this works." Spit flew out of the side of Gulliver's mouth. "Get over it. Everyone in America has had to pay their dues, but do you see any other people crying in their soup? No. Only you guys seem to be stuck in a rut with the ol' gimme syndrome. Fuck all of you and the boats you sailed in on."

"What I don't understand," Stubbs commented calmly, "is why all this venom? You'll have time enough to vent your anger once this is over. The Professor here promised that this sit-down would be cordial."

"Go back to Africa, you black bastard."

Stubbs smiled at Gulliver. "Hmm. That might be a good name for this country."

"Gentlemen," Levy interjected, "this was not intended to be a shouting match although I know emotions are running high on both sides."

"We're cool," Stubbs offered. "It's---."

"I'm going to eat your lunch, Stubbs."

The black lawyer laughed bitterly. "That'll be the day."

It was a full ten minutes before the bickering finally ceased, and once the negotiations did start in earnest, it was inordinately hard for Professor Levy to piece together any workable terms between the two parties. Neither side was even vaguely interested in going half on concessions, and as can be imagined, each wanted the whole hog when it would benefit them. It would have been far simpler, it seemed to Levy, to just let them shoot it out and to be done with it.

"I won't stand for that," East argued vehemently. "It's futile speculation and would be best left up the Judge on that issue. I think we should abide by the Judge's decision."

"Then let's hope he's less of a fool than you," Stubbs retorted, "but I'll stand with that. If the question arises during the course of the trial, we'll defer to whomever presides." He glared at East. "Let there be no tears in the end, buster."

"Nothing else is intercept-free, though. You put it out there and I'm going to stomp on it."

"What about expert witnesses?"

"As long as they're relevant and authentic, fine. I'll object like hell to a carnival." East paused thoughtfully. "He's neutral." He indicated Levy. "Neither of us can use him or anyone associated with him."

"Deal," Stubbs huddled with Peterson. "The next question is how do you intend to edit out or eliminate the charge of the racial duplicity in all this? Everyone is obviously aware of the home-grown racism that sparked the murder."

"I have a big problem with that, mister. The racism of Ol' Miss is not to be put on trial. You pull that shit, and all professional courtesies fly out of the window. You savvy?"

Sensing the atmosphere heating up again, Levy pressed the men on. "We still have a lot of ground to cover, and we need to keep all channels open." He considered the practicality of closing shop now, making good on the promises he had already hammered out on both sides, and then await the fireworks during trial. Levy knew that although neither lawyer would confess it, they would both go far to line up a case that would be over-the-top spectacular. And neither would be modest.

"I would almost bet." East taunted, "that your whole case will revolve around the Amistad case argued by John Quincy Adams in 1841." He smiled knowingly at Stubbs. "Is that a good guess?"

The black lawyer slapped himself upside the head playfully. "The Amistad case? You know, I'd never considered that, but I'm grateful you mentioned it. Thanks for such an incredible piece of law even though I was a bit more lucky in my research. Came up with some shit that will make you lil' white toes curl up like pork rinds."

"You can spew out all the legal garbage you want," Gulliver cracked, "but it still won't help. We don't bluff easy."

"Bluffing was not what I had in mind." Stubbs looked at Levy. "What else is there?"

The Professor sighed heavily. "Considering what the stakes are, the aftermath could be messy, no matter who prevails, I want to insure that---."

"Wait a fucking minute," Stubbs growled. "As I understood it, this is winner-take- all, right?"

"B-but there must be concessions," Levy said nervously. "It's only fair."

Stubbs nudged Congressman Peterson. "I knew where this was headed the moment he started begging for insurance." He frowned at Levy. "No way. There are to be no liabilities attached with winning."

Levy glanced at East who leaned back in his chair as if an answer was beneath his dignity, yet he did respond. "Just like a nigger---."

Peterson flinched, bolted upright. "I'm warning you, ease up with the racist crap."

Stubbs touched the Congressman's arm. "It's okay, brer, I eat crackers like him up and spit 'em out every day of the week, except Saturday and Sunday because that's when I make love to white women." He glared across at Gulliver and East. "I'm damned good at that also."

"But I always thought it was virtually impossible for a monkey to fuck a human being."

"*Gentlemen!*" Levy shouted. "This is getting out of hand. As moderator, I insist on some decorum. We are civilized men here."

Gulliver snickered.

Levy held up his hand to indicate quiet as if he was lecturing in a classroom. "Even though none of what happens in the courtroom or afterwards will ever be released publicly, additional steps, I feel must be taken to insure…parity."

"Such as what?" Stubbs huffed defiantly.

"Such as this," East broke in. "If your guys win, what have you actually lost? Not a damn thing. Life goes on for blacks and they won't miss a beat, but on the other hand, we lose everything."

"So, that's where this parity shit comes in," Stubbs scoffed. "Parity, my ass. Sounds like you guys want to party, win or lose." He faced Levy. "What do they want, to be able to keep all their belongings intact. Whoa now, boys, QuickSilver Properties is a nest egg---."

Gulliver was up and across the table, but both Levy and East managed to restrain him, and to pull him back across to his chair where they worked furiously to calm him down.

"No one is going to lay one fucking finger on QuickSilver," Gulliver ranted. "No fucking body."

Stubbs was unfazed. "Unless you win---."

Gulliver tried to break free. "Get them out of here. Get them out of my sight now."

The black men stood to leave.

"Since you want to play hard ball," Gulliver yelled, "I'll get ugly too. Since you bastards feel it's so cute to gamble when you have nothing to lose, I'll show you just how cute it is. If the white side loses, we lose everything, but if the black side loses, you'll lose your nigger lives, every goddamned one of you. What do you have to say to that?"

"We'll see you in court," Stubbs said firmly, slamming the door on the way out.

TWO

Judge Ervin Roman performed his duties in such a high-handed fashion that little room was left to doubt whose courtroom it was. He loved battles to be fought in his court, but he made sure both sides played from within the same rulebook. He interacted with the attorneys in his courtroom only when either became too absorbed in trying to pull the wool over the eyes of the opposing team. He would let you slug it out, but you couldn't kick 'em when they were down.

Without barely any shouting from the defense team. Judge Roman turned down the request for a change of venue. Officer Rand would eventually face the music in Bolivar County, and he was to remain in custody until such time as trial commenced which would be soon. East's motion for a speedy trial was granted.

During the entire session, there was no talk of compromise or any plea for a reduced charge, so Stubbs was more than vaguely annoyed when East tugged at his sleeve as he exited the courtroom, pressing a crumpled slip of paper into his palm.

"What was that all about?" Congressman Peterson quizzed.

Stubbs stared at East's back as the lawyer sauntered away. "Don't know." He stashed the paper into his jacket pocket. "Let's go. I'll check it out once we're outside."

Crossing the street from the courthouse, Stubbs fished the yellow paper out of his pocket, Peterson close at his elbow. In a script that was, at first, almost unrecognizable, it took maybe a second before Stubbs' eyes were able to follow the movement of the letters and discern their graphic portent.

"Hmm," Stubbs mused

"You   going?"

With no definite clues as to what was up, the note wasn't easy to take in. There was scarcely anything in the inelegant handwriting on the hastily torn out piece of paper that suggested an urgency of any sort, but that, in and of itself, was not comprehensive enough to blur his sense of playing all the angles. This could be important.

"The bastard had ample time this morning to pitch to the Judge if he had an issue," Peterson remarked. "Let him stew."

"Naw, man, what can it hurt?"

"Maurice, you think I don't trust these jokers. I haven't forgotten that my niece is dead because of them."

Stubbs stopped walking and gripped Peterson's arms. "Come on, brer, don't lose focus. It's important that we not give an inch, so I beg you not to confuse the players. East is second string, and had nothing at all to do with the murder of your niece."

"I feel you, brer, "Peterson replied, "but the same motherfucka who is paying the lawyers is the same motherfucka that paid for the hit-man. I was cool at the meeting in North Carolina because you insisted on it, but I could've strangled that Merchant cracker. He's the one, Maurice. I have got to have his ass. For Venus."

"Family honor is one thing, Will, the survival of the whole race, another. Just continue to play along, keep on being cool. Let me take East's best shot and see what he's got. Can you handle that until I get us down in scoring range?"

Peterson nodded.

"Good. Now, let me meet this white boy for coffee."

<<<<<<<<<<<<<<<<<
SOULFIRE BOOKS
<<<<<<<<<<<<<<<<<

"How you take your mud?"

"Black and strong, just like me."

East looked momentarily deflated, then responded caustically. "To be like you, shouldn't you drop in a shovel full of milk. You're quite diluted, if you ask me. Could damn near pass for white if you were any lighter." When the waiter came by, East looked pleased. "I'll like a tall glass of white milk." He stared across at Stubbs. "For my friend, coffee. Make it strong and black, please. That's how you like it, isn't it?"

"What is this all about, East, that's the real question? I don't have much time for any sideshows."

"Eager for the Big-Top, huh?"

The beverages arrived. Neither man touched his.

"I would think that by now you should have seen the futility of your position and well, you know how it goes. You're an old soldier, Stubbs, and you've given as good as you've got, but this time, you're in outer space where there's not enough oxygen to sustain your case. Give it up, Stubbs. Your position is brain dead."

"Funny, but I was thinking that exact same thing about your end of this issue. I mean, you would have to realize that you can't win this even in your wildest dreams."

Silence, and then East sipped his milk. "I've beat the bushes on both ends of this tug-of-war and it comes up short from where you stand." East smiled. "And even the best of us can't make a case out of nothing at all." Still smiling, he set the milk down. "That being so, isn't it time you considered other options?" Again, he quickly added. "I'm well aware of your reputation as well as your fierce competitiveness, but then I'm no slouch myself, but that is neither here nor there, my esteemed colleague---."

"What your pitch, East?"

"Let's say that you concede right now."

"What if I did, hypothetically speaking?"

"Then I'd be happy as hell to be generous to you. In that case, and acting on behalf of the Merchant family, mind you, I'd be in a position to not only lift the threat of violence, but also to make other concessions."

"In addition to saving the entire black race!? Other concessions. Why, that's almost unimaginable." Stubbs mimicked mockingly.

"This is not the time to be funny, Stubbs, and time is pressing."

"Well, in that case, East, on behalf of all the niggers in the world, kiss my ass." The venom is Stubbs voice was so repulsive it startled East so much that when he pulled back, he almost toppled his glass of milk over.

"You'll regret this, Stubbs. That's a promise."

"Just like the 40 acres and a mule; just like civil rights, just like separate but equal---."

"I'm warning you to reconsider for your won damned good."

Stubbs leaned forward. "This god complex you white people have boggles my mind, always thinking you know what's right for black people, and then threatening brimstone and fire if we don't kiss your white asses in appreciation." He dropped a dollar on the table as he stood to leave. "Go tell your boss that this is one dream we're not buying." He strolled off.

"Stubbs!"

The black man stopped, turned, walked the few steps back to the table. He clasped his hands behind his back demurely. "On second thought, there is something you can do for me. Sadly, I don't have any white women lined up for this weekend, and I was wondering what your wife and daughter are doing this Saturday and Sunday."

THREE

They ranged in age from their mid-twenties to their late sixties, and among them were a janitor, a bank teller, a right-wing Christian, and a wannabe Mack Daddy with his gold tooth flashing. They all sat straight, looking out into the courtroom, feeling slightly superior now that they had been selected for jury duty in the biggest trial ever in Bolivar County. Murder!

Stubbs measured them carefully as did East. They sure as hell were not a jazz combo, but they did look like they had all been plucked from a Benetton ad, so maybe they would have no trouble thinking in concert with one another.

"Well," East whispered in a low, guttural voice to a female member of the defense team, "let the fun begin."

Stubbs was more reserved, but his eye continued to roam the jury box even though it was now a done deal. These were the people who had just been given final say of the future of America.

East, clean-shaven and in a sparkling new blue linen suit, looked decidedly conservative. His demeanor was severely professional, a man-in-charge, in total control, but he still floated a silent prayer to the heavens as he half-listened to the Judge admonish, well, actually threaten, the jury. He warned them not to discuss the trial with anyone, or to read anything about it, or to watch anything about it on TV. Then after thanking them in advance for services not yet rendered, he surprised everyone with a long recess.

Court would resume in the morning, Thursday the 15th.

<<<<<<<<<<<<<<<
SOULFIRE BOOKS
<<<<<<<<<<<<<<<

Night had seemed to serve no function at all, and the only special feature about it had been the fact that it was over with so quickly Stubbs had no time to ponder long and hard about what daybreak would usher in. Already the morning, though still young, radiated with an uncommon strength, and since there certainly had to be some truth in what Roosevelt had said about fear, Stubbs couldn't subdue or conquer his. To the near exclusion of everything else, he felt fear, the power of it quite stronger than his immunity against it. Even though he was intimately familiar with the origin of the dread, this exceptional clarity afforded him nothing in the way of an emotional hook whereby he could grapple with this mental menace. But doubt played a role also, abbreviating him, watering him down.

Stubbs, nonetheless, was morbidly fascinated at what could possibly happen next, but at a little after eight o'clock, he screwed on his game face and headed out. The bullshit was over, He was off to war.

SOULFIRE BOOKS

Adapting himself to novel situations did not run counter to what East had done practically all his life, so he faced the morning with a composed serenity. The earlier doubts and vacillations were gone, and he was now determined to win, and he wouldn't refrain from playing dirty if the situation dictated because his case had to be ruthlessly presented. This was both the exception and the rule.

However, nothing would be more satisfying than the joy he would get from beating Maurice Stubbs in court. Such a victory would validate him, would prove his ultimate worth, but he marveled at just how devastating his win would be to Stubbs and the rest of black America, but that wasn't his cross to bear. What happened--- happened. And with that thought in mind, East mentally brought all the complexities of his character into a single resolve, and then headed out. The bullshit was over. He was off to war.

SOULFIRE BOOKS

9:00am. Bolivar County Courthouse. Thursday.

When Stubbs stood up to make his opening statement, everything felt positively surreal. It was as though the cavernous jury box was inhabited not with humans, but with ghosts and phantoms. They were so clear, yet so unreal, and he had little or nothing in his experiences to compare this specter with. Still, he had to prevail, and he couldn't wait and to see what would happen if he did nothing. His number had been called so they awaited him, inspecting him. Sizing him up.

"Ladies and gentlemen of the jury," he commenced with a naturalness he didn't feel, "good morning." Then his voice broke up. The audience leaned forward, wanting to see what risks he would take with them. Stubbs was dismayed, but every fiber of his being silently shored him up until he started to feel unbreakable. Internally propped-up with spiritual backbone, he imposed calm on himself, and smoothly explained the mechanics of his mission. The jury hung onto his every word as he careened from one point to the next, but the honeymoon didn't last long because it clearly frustrated the jury when he attempted to paint in the racist color of the killing. He knew he had touched a nerve. Ole Miss had struggled for decades trying to live down its racist past, and didn't need a Yankee prosecutor to remind them of their faults.

Meanwhile, East smiled as he saw his adversary blow his chance to zoom to an early lead. Murder was one thing, transforming racists was another. East continued to smile, praying that Stubbs wouldn't recover from that apparent error.

"No city has a monopoly on the murder of innocent, young, black boys, but what happened here in Bolivar County was wrong, dead wrong." Stubbs' approach softened once he saw the need to assure the jury he was not some glory-seeking outsider who lacked the good sense to understand their inherited pain and embarrassment. "The hallmark of what happened here to young Tony Rawls is not a throw-back to the old segregated Mississippi. No, this murder has nothing to do with that. It has everything to do with now, right now. Today. Tony Rawls was gunned down in cold-blood, but he wasn't trying to integrate anything, so let's be upfront about that. All Tony Rawls wanted to do that night was to go home, and in America, how big a crime is that? How can anyone go wrong wanting to go home? To Tony Rawls, home was where Mama was, and wonder of wonders, Papa also. Here was a boy, able to grow up minus the turbulence of being reared in an one-parent household, and just when it seemed it couldn't get any better, police officer Rand gunned him down."

East had encountered this way of thinking before, so nothing being said worried him. He understood Stubbs' objective and knew the odds of him reaching it, but what he didn't know was how far the black lawyer would go to shake things up. This realization compelled East to pay closer attention to the proceedings. He needed to know precisely what it was that Stubbs was trying to sell.

By now, Stubbs was laying it on thick. He was standing directly in front of the jury box. "I want to infuse all of you with a single goal, but first," he whispered softly, "I want to let you in on a little secret." He glanced furtively at East as though he was the scum of the earth, and then nervously turned back to face the jury. He drew them in his confidence. "It is universally known that in a murder trial certain commonplace elements must be proved, you know, elementary things such as motive, intent, and opportunity." He winked at the juror. "That's how it is normally done, but not this time. Not here in the wonderful state of Mississippi. Instead of establishing those three elements," he enumerated each one slowly. "For some reason, the defense says that, all of a sudden, motive, intent, and opportunity are not enough of a basis to demonstrate that Officer Rand committed a heinous killing. They demand more."

East's body went rigid, and he sat ram-rod straight. Stubbs was about to announce and unveil their secret strategy, the legal framework on which they both would build their case. East was feeling dizzy because if not presented right, this could become an obstacle, an unsurmountable sticking point that would doom them both, and the trial they planned might not get off the ground.

East could barely contain his anxiety, but to his credit, he remained composed. "Yikes," he muttered under his voice, realizing that very few defense lawyers delighted in hearing the prosecutor make a point. "Go for it, you bastard," East muttered breathless. He sure as hell didn't want to have to do the bastard's job for him.

"It's very sad, this extra mile you've been asked to travel, but I get the feeling that this is the right jury for the job. No matter what," Stubbs winked, "they sure chose the right jury to pick on." Stubbs walked back over to his table, and rummaged through some papers. "This is new to me, also," he confided over his shoulder. He walked slowly across the well of the courtroom. "As if jury duty wasn't hard enough on its own…and now this. Anyway, the defense in an effort to bolster their inane contention that Officer Rand is totally, completely innocent will insist that no crime was committed because---get this---because Tony Rawls was not a real citizen. I know, I know," Stubbs said pleadingly, "let's not criticize the defense for trying. They're clutching at straws, and in an effort to save their case, that was the best they could do, and even this, this foolishness is not that strong because all of us today know that Tony Rawls was an American citizen. Yet the lawyers for the accused are going to argue that the beloved 14th Amendment was a hoax, and that, by extension, it never conferred citizenship upon the black freedmen or their subsequent offspring. Isn't that remarkable, but that's what they want you to believe because if they can somehow trick you into believing this, then the murder of Tony Rawls can be wiped away, but I know you won't let that happen, will you? Tony Rawls was an American citizen, and he was murdered, and I say that justice must be done."

East relaxed. It had been particularly challenging, but the fix was in, and although that didn't mean smooth sailing from this point on, the legal spinoff they both desired was now in place. That piece of judicial hocus pocus had earned them the right to disrupt the legal process by stealth, by hook, and by crook, anything to give them an edge in inventing a new American future; a visible monolith where either one race or the other would be missing.

"No one really leaves here with fond memories of jury duty," Stubbs concluded, "but don't underestimate the value of what you're doing, especially in this highly unusual circumstance. I urge you to stay alert, remain vigilant, and to render the truth by convicting the man that killed an American citizen. Thank you."

<<<<<<<<<<<<<<<<<
SOULFIRE BOOKS
<<<<<<<<<<<<<<<<<

When it was East's time to address the jury, he hustled across the courtroom like he couldn't wait to tell the jury what was on his mind, and he did it in such a heated rush that everyone got the impression that what he had to say was indeed important. "I'm honored to say that during my life, I haven't planted many flags, but when I do, you better bet it's a flag worth planting, but first, good morning. Please excuse my ill manners, but we have a big problem on our hands, and I say we jump in and do our collective duty. Now, don't get me wrong because I'm not asking you to plant any flags. That's my job, but I do want you to listen up."

Stubbs looked directly behind him at the Rawls' family to assure them that he could handle anything East said, and for them to remain stoic. Don't send the jury any sign that the defense is getting to you, his glance seemed to say. Yet when it came to being cool, he wasn't that good a poster-child because he still had a serious case of butterflies-in-the-gut.

"At issue," East lectured, "is murder and it is a terribly despicable crime, but it just doesn't end there because this is about the constitution, and though the prosecutor is trying to make this quack like a duck, I say it isn't one. I know how unprecedented this is, be we've been wallowing in legal quicksand long enough so I can plant my flag. What I'm telling you is that the American Constitution is not mere intellectual property where you can take out a patent and add to it as you see fit. Not our constitution, and when I say our constitution, I refer to the beloved document that existed before all the post-it notes, the so-called Amendments." East smiled. "You know what an Amendment is? It's like when you name your son Bob and I decide to call him Charlie. It's not my place to tamper with the right you have given your son, and it wouldn't be good for him if I did so. You know why? Because simply put, it's confusing as the dickens, and that's what the fools who interpret the constitution loosely look to do to us---confuse us, but those who feel that a strict interpretation of the constitution is what the Founding Fathers intended are the smart ones. It's time we started heeding them."

For the next thirty minutes, East patiently lectured that a new dawn was just on the horizon, how prosperity and boom times were now within their grasp, how all they had to do would be to dive bravely into the uncharted waters before them, and choke the life out of the 14th Amendment. He spoke gallantly on how bright the morn would be when the big, bad 14th Amendment was no longer either a business partner or an erring lover in the affairs of the common folk.

"So the next time you wonder where all the uncertainties have come from or why you feel thwarted in your pursuit of life, liberty, and happiness. I'll tell you why. "It's the dag-blamed 14th Amendment. Get rid of it and regain the flexibility to hope and to dream again."

Before concluding, East warned of the danger of complacency, broadly explaining that the jury had the duty to sweep away the 14th Amendment since it was a threat to national security."

Stubbs reckoned that everything he was hearing was inevitable and he could sense that, at the moment, East was stalling, fearful of presenting his far-fetched theory that blacks would be better off without the protection of the 14th Amendment. Stubbs smiled, wondering how East would approach that.

East took a few steps away from the jury box and warily eyed the three black jurors. "The truth is that we, as a people, have never learned how to evaluate the value to tell the truth." His voice sounded sad. "I am no enemy of freedom," he lamented. "I am no racist. You'll see. Thank you."

The Judge banged the gavel. "Recess."

FOUR

"Objection!"

The judge glared at Stubbs. "Sustained."

At the beginning of the trial, Stubbs had little difficulty dictating the pace of the proceeding as East showed hardly any interest in the internal stuffing of the case, but now as he tried to introduce witnesses to widen his 14th Amendment claims, there was much stiffer resistance.

"Now, Professor Welch, according to your studies and supported by law, isn't it a cinch to say that ten years or so after the infamous ruling in Sandford versus Scott, the 14th Amendment legally abolished all constitutional impediments to black citizenship?"

"That is absolutely correct," the dark-skinned professor huffed. "The 14th Amendment totally abrogated the Dred Scott verdict. Thank God."

Stubbs grinned. "I have no further questions, your Honor."

East was on his feet at once. "Professor Welch, am I to understand that what the 14th Amendment did was, what did my esteemed colleague say---ah yes, abolish all the constitutional impediments to black citizenship?"

"Again," Welch replied testily, "the answer is yes."

"I see," East continued. "but isn't it equally true that all the 14th Amendment did, in actuality, was simply to remove the impediments?"

"I don't understand the gist---?"

"At any rate, Mister Welch, no matter how much the good ole' 14th Amendment makes your head swell up---."

"Objection, Your Honor!" Stubbs shouted. "He's belittling the witness, and it's uncalled for."

Judge Roman glared at East.

"Your Honor, no disrespect to the witness, but it is obvious from his earlier testimony that he derives a great deal of pride from the 14th Amendment, and I was basically capitalizing on that fact."

"Overruled."

"Thank you, Judge Roman." Turning back to Professor Welch, East's smile dimmed. "Wouldn't you tend to agree that your beloved 14th Amendment was a tight-fisted, little rascal. I mean it was efficient only, at most, in removing impediments to citizenship, but it stopped and died in its tracks after that, now didn't it? Isn't it true that the 14th Amendment couldn't impose US citizenship upon the newly freed slaves?"

"Impose?" Welch snorted disdainfully.

East stepped back, clutching his chest as if he was startled. "Why, yes, impose, Professor. Come on, now, admit it. You do know what that word means."

"What is this, sir, a trial or Dictionary 101?"

East ignored the remark. "No matter what you claim, and it appears you have good reason to conceal---."

"Are you calling me a liar?!" Welch roared.

"Calm down, Professor, no big deal. I apologize. What's more, I'm going to shorten my cross-examination, but first I need you to tell me if or not the 14th Amendment made citizenship for blacks a choice?" He cupped his ear as if he might have trouble hearing the answer.

Spitefully, the Professor shook his head.

East stormed to the front of the Judge's bench. "Your Honor, would you please direct the witness to answer verbally---and loudly---for the record."

"Answer the question."

"I do not believe that to be true," Welch responded tersely. "No."

"*No!*" East said incredulously. "Explain no to me."

"*Objection*! He's badgering the witness. No is no. What further explanation does defense desire—or deserve?"

"Sustained."

East ambled back to the defense table, mumbling to himself. He fumbled noisily through his briefcase. "Aha," he exclaimed happily, "here's one." He flapped the paper like it was a flag. He smiled. "Now, let's see what happens. According to this, the first section of the 14th Amendment which was ratified in 1868, declared that all persons born or naturalized in the United States and subject to the jurisdiction thereof, are US citizens." He glared at Welch. "Were blacks in 1868 lawfully subject to US jurisdiction?"

Welch spoke softly. "No."

"No?"

"But section two gave Congress the right to eliminate all shades, conditions, badges, and incidents of slavery." Welch sounded smug. "The Benevolent Protector Clause."

"So, what you mean is that Uncle Sam was looking out for the black race. Is that what you're saying?"

"Exactly."

"Yet the imposition of US citizenship on blacks who did not choose it, or voluntarily accept it, would constitute a government action which was unlawful since it would be imposing upon blacks. Isn't it true that just like it was unlawful to impose slavery upon the black race, it was equally unlawful to impose citizenship upon them because this would deny them the willful freedom to choose, wouldn't it?"

"I feel it would be useless to speculate---."

"Forget speculation, Professor, what I'm asking is that to the best of your knowledge and belief, isn't it true that unless blacks chose US citizenship, the Civil Rights Act of 1866 and the 14th Amendment which brought about the legal basis of that choice would not apply?"

"I-I don't know about that."

"You don't know."

"That's what I said. I don't know."

"Well, how does this sound? Blacks were never naturalized, and they never chose citizenship. How does that sound?"

"Like I want to be dismissed."

"He's ready to go, Your Honor, and I don't feel it would be fair to impose upon the Professor as this would circumvent his choice, and since I don't practice tyranny, I conclude my cross."

"You're dismissed," the Judge commented.

<<<<<<<<<<<<<<<<
SOULFIRE BOOKS
<<<<<<<<<<<<<<<<

"We didn't bother with that, sir. It's standard procedure."

"It is?" Stubbs pretended astonishment. "But how do you identify them?"

Timothy Hanks, paramedic, looked surprised, his expression conveying how much. "If you mean, do we go through their personal effects, we don't do that."

"I recognize that, but how would you know if the person…..one moment, please." Stubbs sauntered over to his table and picked up a written report. "Checking this log, I find your signature. That is your handwriting right there, isn't it?"

"Yes."

"Okay, good. So, it's my guess that on that evening when you," Stubbs lowered his voice, "when you arrived at the crime scene and picked up the body of Tony Rawls, you automatically assumed what, that you were picking up the body of an American citizen?"

Hanks shrugged. "He was dead, but still just as American as anyone else I'd ever seen."

"So there was never any question of his citizenship? As far as you could tell, the body did not belong to some stateless person?"

"No."

<<<<<<<<<<<<<<<<
SOULFIRE BOOKS
<<<<<<<<<<<<<<<<

"When you implied that Mister Rawls did not appear stateless," East countered, "just what did you mean? Have you ever, by chance, seen a stateless person?"

"I don't check passports."

"In that case, for all you know, Mister Rawls, as opposed to being stateless, could have been have been a citizen of one of the many African nation, or even from Cuba or somewhere in Haiti, for all you know since you don't check passports. To be honest, Mister Hanks, on that night you picked up a dead body, isn't that right?"

"That is correct, sir."

"And you had no immediate way of identifying that body as an American citizen, now did you?"

"Objection! Calls for speculation on the part of the witness."

"Overruled."

"What I'm asking," East continued, "is if you even attempt to identify a body as a citizen or not?"

"No,"

"So, you don't know if he was stateless or not?"

"No."

"Thanks," East sighed, "that takes a load off."

<<<<<<<<<<<<<<<<

SOULFIRE BOOKS

<<<<<<<<<<<<<<<<<

It was moderately cold the next morning in the courtroom on Tuesday, and the jury appeared to be huddled together for extra warmth. Stubbs gave them a heated blast of a smile as he took the floor after the witness had been sworn in. Warming his voice up, he politely solicited some preliminary background info on the witness, and then casually tossed him a short shopping list of leading questions. "And?"

"Most importantly, the informed observation is that it laid the Dred Scott decision to rest because no doubt the 14th Amendment was intended to admit the black race into citizenship."

"Let me point something out. It's a wee bit puzzling to me, so I need help." Stubbs smiled. "I'm only a lawyer, but you're a famous professor, so here's my question. When you said the 14th Amendment intended to admit blacks into citizenship, did you mean state citizenship, national citizenship, or both?"

"Both. Residence in a state makes you a citizen of that state, but to be a citizen of the nation, all that is necessary is that one be born or naturalized here."

"I see, so the Privileges and Immunities of the 14th Amendment are fundamentally sound and are enjoyed by citizens of all the states no matter where they reside in the Union. Correct?"

"Correct."

"It must follow, then, from what you're telling me, that as a citizen, Tony Rawls had rights that must be protected by the state of Mississippi. For instance, if Tony Rawls, as a citizen was murdered, the state of Mississippi could legally draw up charges and issue an indictment for murder?"

"Of course. One of the privileges of a citizen in this country is to have the care and protection of both the state and national government over his life."

Stubbs faced the jury as he spoke. "Can we quote you on that, Professor, because, if so, that means---well it means a lot. The mere fact that the state of Mississippi drew up an indictment in the murder of Tony Rawls evidently suggests that he was viewed as a bonafide citizen." Stubbs turned back to the witness. "If Tony Rawls had not been a citizen, then it would have been useless to pursue an indictment on his behalf, wouldn't it?"

"Of this, there is no doubt, sir. If Mister Rawls had lacked citizenship, then no warrant would have issued since Mister Rawls and all blacks would have still been under the care of the Dred Scott decision."

Stubbs walked up to the witness box. "If you'll give us some background information on this Dred Scott case, we would appreciate it."

The witness sighed. "What's to tell, but in a nutshell, it boiled down legally to a view that citizenship of the United States was dependent upon citizenship in any of the several states that made up the Union."

Stubbs looked at each juror. "Was there a problem with that, Professor?"

"A big one, sir, A damnable one. You see, if there was no citizenship independent of that of the states, then blacks could not technically be real citizens---."

"Whoa," Stubbs exclaimed, spinning around, "that's amazing. Good thing the 14th Amendment put that right."

Walking slowly back to his table, he wondered what East would do on cross-examination, and the mere thought of that soon-to-be answered question almost made a cold chill run up his spine.

For Stubbs, up until this morning, he had believed in the half-cocked notion that no lawyer could slow him down in the courtroom, but East's strategy had him ready to look beyond that far-fetched assumption. Over the last week, East had matched him stride for stride, and Stubbs knew that he couldn't afford to allow the case to stay so close. He had to blow East's ass out of the water---or else. It was time for him to secure a decided advantage. Or else. And it wasn't like he was playing it safe or practicing legal conservatism. It was just that East was effectively blocking and check-mating him, and now was surely not the time for that shit.

The stability of his case was still unusually strong even though his synchronicity was weirdly off-kilter. This only meant that he would have to construct a more proactive approach to support his core premise that Tony Rawls---and hence all blacks---possessed citizenship rights. Specifically, since there was no way to take the thunder out of this premise, he should have no concerns about either risk avoidance or risk management, but the stakes were too high for carelessness. This would be an interesting case of playing it by ear without sometimes being able to hear the music.

Stubbs felt good with himself just the same.

SOULFIRE BOOKS

That evening, immediately upon receiving the Judge's orders to commence his cross-examination, East flanked he witness stand, not getting close as though it was electrified. "Hello," he said pleasantly. "Now, let me get this right. At the time of Dred Scott, it was legally accepted that there was no citizenship independent of state citizenship, right?"

"Yes," the witness nodded.

East nodded approvingly. "Then what the 14th Amendment did was to invent, for the first time in our history, national citizens. Before the 14th Amendment, the idea of national citizens conjured up by the government was preposterous. As a matter of fact, the newly freed slaves were unofficially the first and only so-called, quote unquote, national citizens, correct?"

"I would imagine," the witness said weakly."

"I would imagine also," East mimicked. "How else could it have been? Whites in this country had God-given, inalienable right secured under the 6th Amendment which, by the way, was an original part of the Constitution. So then, just for the sake of argument, let's say that in 1868, blacks became brand new members of the national government, but were they actual citizens?" East shook his head stiffly. "No, and you know why? They were never made, by extension, citizens of any state." He strolled away, talking to the witness over his shoulder. "In fact, the exclusive privilege of citizenship was a grant of the states, and the 14th Amendment lacked the authority to transfer this power to the national government." He stood in place at his table and glared at the witness accusingly. "Isn't it true that the notion of anyone being a citizen of the United States was laughed at?"

The witness squirmed, looking at Stubbs for help.

"Answer the question, please." East demanded.

"That was true, but---.'

"Yes," East shouted. "Or no."

"Yes."

East relaxed. "Isn't it also a celebrated fact that most members of Congress didn't cotton to the concept that there could be, in this country, any such thing as a citizen at-large, one whose citizenship extended to the whole geography of the nation?" East smiled. "Isn't it even true that a senator at that time declared in a famous speech that such a national citizen would be a perfect nondescript, and that not a single individual of this description could be found anywhere? He went on to say that a citizen is a citizen of some State, and it is he who is under the provisions of the Constitution. Am I right or wrong?"

"You're right."

East spoke to the jury. "There you have it. Only white people who were citizens of their respective States were protected by the Constitution. It's sad I know, but since it was not in the power of any State to invest the black man with real citizenship, he could not enjoy the privileges of a flesh and blood citizen under the Constitution because no black person could be a citizen within the meaning of the Constitution. He flung his body around quickly. He grinned at the witness. "Tell me I' wrong?"

"When the blacks were naturalized, we----."

"I'm finished with this witness, Your Honor."

<<<<<<<<<<<<<<<<
SOULFIRE BOOKS
<<<<<<<<<<<<<<<<<

On redirect, Stubbs knew he had to pull his ass up from the ashes. He wasn't particularly thrilled at the mess East had made for him, but he had to cue up the jury that naturalization of the former slaves was some sort of constitutional gentlemen's agreement between the state and national governments that permitted blacks the common fare to enjoy equal protection under the law.

By almost every legal yardstick, this redirect had to be a big departure from his direct examination if he was going to elicit the fabulous testimony he needed to put a foot in East's mouth.

"I know you're tired, Professor," Stubbs cracked, "but this is important. Then we'll let you go, okay."

The witness smiled glumly.

East relaxed. There was not enough applause in the naturalization angle to worry him, so it didn't matter how much it was souped-up, it wouldn't change the outcome of the info he'd extracted. Oh God, East thought. He had enjoyed pulling those teeth. What a boost to his confidence.

As he lazily watched Stubbs propel himself towards the jury box, he suddenly felt like a shrinking violet because no matter how much he cannibalized Stubbs' arguments, he still had to deal with the unfortunate presence of the blacks on the jury, and he widely regarded it as a legal disaster of damned near catastrophic proportions. He privately lamented the fact that he hadn't found the means to get all their black asses dismissed because how, for crying out loud, did he get them to cozy up to the belief that they were not real citizens. East winced in pain. And just how crazy was that going to be? After all, here their nigger asses sat on an empaneled jury, and didn't the fucking law state that only legal citizens could perform jury duty.

Shit, Gulliver was going to have to commit some murders.

FIVE

"I don't see why not?" East yelled. "It's not like it's unannounced or anything. Your fucking antenna should've gone up the minute you saw I was stuck with those niggers for jurors. Shit, what did you expect?"

Gulliver peered wearily out of eyes ringed with dark circles, and red with swollen puffiness. "And you want them all---."

"What the hell do you think?" East was livid. "There is no fucking way I can win those bastards over," he groaned. "I can't lose this case. I can't."

"Dammit, East," Gulliver snarled angrily. "Have you forgotten what's going on? This is not about you and Stubbs, remember? It's bigger than that. So let's get back on track."

"Then you have got to houseclean. Get rid of the jungle-bunnies and I'll win one for the home team." East's voice became conciliatory. "Let's be reasonable. It doesn't matter how pretty or high a brick wall I build, I don't see the blacks returning a verdict declaring that they are stateless." East drew a deep breath. "I don't think that will happen, doc."

Gulliver placed a reassuring hand on East's shoulder. "They're niggers. Just separate them from the rest of the proceedings. Make them feel that this is not about them, but all about Tony Rawls, and that the outcome won't have any adverse effect on them."

East laughed. "And you really believe that bullshit, don't you? How smart do you have to be to put two and two together? Your scenario won't work. Let me explain why."

"Okay, okay," Gulliver rasped, "what do you want done?"

"Now, you're talking," East chuckled. "Now, you're talking."

<<<<<<<<<<<<<<<
SOULFIRE BOOKS
<<<<<<<<<<<<<<<<

The next day. In Court.
After the insipid extravaganza of swearing in the alternate juror, East stole a peek at Stubbs to see how much he enjoyed the

recycled look of the jury. For starters, the expression on the black man's face was as rabid as if he'd discovered that someone had dumped sugar in his gas tank. East couldn't conceal his glee even though he knew it beamed the message: *"You ain't seen nuthin' yet!"*

Despite the fact that Judge Roman never disclosed why the juror was absent or what had happened to her, it didn't matter to East who knew the psychological tweak would unsettle Stubbs. Although the loss of a single, black juror wouldn't be cause enough for Stubbs to slash his wrists, it would indeed call for some adjustments, especially since the missing black, female juror was the one Stubbs had eating out of his hands, and there was no disputing that she was the one he had zeroed in on to carry the banner for him during deliberations.

Excellent choice, East thought as he locked eyes briefly with Gulliver, who sat two rows back in a three thousand dollar suit. Obviously, Gulliver tried to look as though he wasn't the perfect fit for whatever shenanigans had gone down, but the passion of it still twinkled around the corners of his eyes.

Moments later when Stubbs arose from his seat to start his direct, it was evident he wasn't feeling well, and that he was prepared to trim off all the fat from his case and to gnaw on the bone. East was not overly shocked at the not-so-subtle implication. With only a couple of exceptions, East felt that, at the moment, he was the very best lawyer on the planet. Of course, it never hurt to have powerful friends like Gulliver Merchant, especially when you needed to throw a bucket of cold water on your opponent's case just as soon as it started to heat up.

"Mister Chalmers," Stubbs began informally, "as an expert on the constitution, I'd like you to answer this question. Were the fundamental right, privileges, and immunities given to a citizen dependent upon his citizenship of any State? Answer that for me, if you would please."

"No."

"You may elaborate," Stubbs prodded. "Continue."

"With the passage of the 14th Amendment, a citizen of a State now, in effect, became a citizen of the United States who resided in a particular State. In essence, he became a United States citizen as well a resident of his home State."

"So, the 14th Amendment dissolved State citizenship?"

"Yes. The States no longer contained citizens, only residents. Not only this, but the rights, privileges, and immunities which belonged to him as a State's citizen also now belonged to him as a national citizen."

"Tell me something else. Could the State, any State, do anything to affect these rights now held by the national citizen?"

"No. The 14th Amendment likewise forbade any State legislation that abridged these secured rights."

East half-tuned Stubbs out because this line of questioning represented much of what he would hear for the next twenty minutes. He'd let Stubbs take a few more bites out of the apple, and then toss in a few objections to disrupt his rhythm. Inevitably, he knew that on his cross-examination, he would have to backtrack Chalmers through a good deal of his patented song-and-dance to install a reasonable doubt about his veracity, but if that didn't work, he still had a trick or two he could use to destroy the morale of a star prosecution witness.

<<<<<<<<<<<<<<<<
SOULFIRE BOOKS
<<<<<<<<<<<<<<<<

"Yes, yes, yes," Stubbs spouted in rhapsodic ecstasy. It was now mid-morning and he was energized, bouncing around like a gangsta rapper in concert. "Would you mind if I asked you to name for me a couple of those rights that couldn't be abridged? Could you do that?"

"Sure. The declared privileges and immunities or at least a portion of them, included the right to make and enforce contracts, to sue----."

"*Whooeee!*" Stubbs exclaimed, "Go ahead, please. Don't mind me, I'm just feeling it."

East leaped to his feet. "Your Honor, I object to all the theatrics. I see no reason or cause for them."

"Great testimony moves me, Your Honor."

"Overruled."

Stubbs begged his witness to continue, all the while carrying on as if the news was spiritually transforming his life. His contrived rapture was so compelling that by now several jurors had picked up his habit of swaying back and forth as the witness counted off his list of rights. Whether or not, he had successfully wooed these jurors or if they were just caught up in the Sunday morning fever of his legal gospel would remain open to question, but Stubbs knew now was the time to drill for oil. "So that pretty much meant that this extended the protection of the national government to the common right of State's citizens?"

"That is true. It was now set out that all persons born in the United States would be entitled to the rights of citizens."

"Every one of them?"

"That's what all means, doesn't it? Everyone."

SOULFIRE BOOKS

East's cross-examination of the witness was based upon the model of his earlier questioning, but he felt it was now time to destroy the underlying principle of Stubbs' case, and by so tampering with the claim's mortality, to render all the other prosecutorial evidence implausible.

It was just before the time for noon recess when East sauntered up to the witness box as casually as he would the counter in his favorite bar, and stared into the eyes of the witness. "There is something that plagues me like an itch I can't scratch. You know what that is? Of course, you don't," he answered himself, "so I'll tell you. I wasn't going to say anything about it. I'm just like that sometimes. You know, just let stuff pass. Well, anyway, I thought to myself—why not? With all this talk about those rights and man, that was quite a laundry list. Tell you what, and I pray to Jesus that I don't get carried away like my esteemed colleague did, but would you, would you mind just repeating those rights again. There is just, well, what I'm saying is that you have this magical way of naming stuff." East smiled. "I bet you hear that all the time. Man, I bet when you count off the ways you love your wife, I just can imagine what it does too her…Wow!"

"*Objection*! Irrelevant as to his wife."

"Sustained."

"I apologize, Your Honor, but his voice is a national treasure. In all my days on this green earth, I have never heard anyone run down a list with such-such warmth and beauty."

"Counselor, carry on." The Judge rolled his eyes.

East looked like he was afraid, "Wait a minute," he pleaded with the witness. "Give me the chance to get back way over here by my table before you start. I don't think any man should stand that close to such a voice. It's like a choir of angels---."

"*Counselor!*"

East darted to his table. "Let her rip. I feel safe now."

"The rights were as such as to make and enforce contracts, to sue----."

"*Whooeee!*" East yelled.

"*Objection!*"

"What? He did it, Your Honor, and now I know why. That voice."

"Overruled,"

"To be parties in court and to give evidence, to inherit, purchase, lease, sell, hold, and convey real and personal property."

"Black folks as well as whites?"

"Yes sir."

"Well, I'll be. Go on, proceed. No, on second thought, shut up and listen."

"*Objection!* He's bullying the witness, Your Honor."

"Sustained."

Stubbs watched warily as East approached the witness stand because now East strutted like a conquering hero, so unlike earlier. "What a piece of work," East spat meanly. "Who do you think you are?"

"*Objection!* Counselor is out of line, Your Honor."

"Sustained. I'm warning you, Counselor East."

It was as if East hadn't heard. "You're so full of bull----."

"*Objection!* Stubbs was on his feet, yelling and pointing at East. "He's gone overboard. He's crossed the line. He-he's lost his mind, Your Honor."

Judge Roman banged the gavel loudly, declaring a recess, and summoning the attorneys to his chambers.

SOULFIRE BOOKS

After lunch, East was unrepentant. He took the floor and walked to within a few feet of the witness stand. "Remember me?" he asked threateningly.

Stubbs braced himself to spring up and to object, but East walked away.

"The thing I find myself asking is why is it so hard to tell the Court….What was that list again?"

"My God!" Stubbs shouted heatedly. "Here we go again. It's entered into the record."

"Sustained. Must I remind you of our little talk, Counselor East?"

East turned away from the witness in apparent disgust, focusing on the jurors. "Why couldn't he have told you?" he moaned. "Why?"

Both Stubbs and the Judge were ready. Stubbs to object, and Judge Roman to sustain it with a resounding thud of his gavel.

East's tone grew remorseful as he dropped his head in mournful contrition. "I-I can't deny it." He pointed at the witness. "He was right. I won't lie. When he testified, under oath, that the 14th Amendment prohibited a State from depriving any person of life, liberty, or property without due process of law, he was absolutely, one hundred percent correct, but what I find so despicable is that he failed to mention that this added nothing to the rights of one citizen against another." He held up his hand in a stopping motion. "Wait a minute. Hold on. I don't mean to say that it is all right to go out and to do ugly things to each other like murder, but what I do say is that the duty of protecting all its citizens was originally assured by the States, and this never changed. The only obligation the United States had was to see to it that the States did not deny these rights. Nothing more. The government could guarantee this right, but not enforce it because the rights of one citizen against another was a State issue, right?"

"Well----."

"For the protection of that one, single right, the people had to look to the States, didn't they?"

"In a manner of speaking, yes."

"Yes, he said," East bellowed. "Yes!" He squared his shoulders and confronted the jury. "And guess what, black people were never State citizens. They were nationals of the government which mean they lacked this most vital right to be protected from other citizens since they were stateless---."

"Naturalization solved that," the witness retorted.

East stopped, flinging his body around in a full circle. "What did you say?"

"Naturalization---."

East burst out laughing. "Okay, okay," he chortled, "let's see about that. Tell me about naturalization. Was that something like natural childbirth, by the way?"

Stubbs was on his feet, but before he could object, the Judge had issued a stern warning.

The witness stared at the Judge. "May I begin by going back to the 13th Amendment to help explain myself?"

Judge Roman glanced at East.

"Why the hell not," East answered grandly. "I'm a pussy-cat."

Judge Roman's face reddened considerably, but he didn't chastise the lawyer. "You may proceed," he informed the witness.

"On second thought," East growled before the witness spoke. "I'm having second thoughts about this 13th Amendment party pack. He dashed over to the jury box. "And you know why? It's a crock of doo-doo."

"Objection!"

"Sustained! One more crack like that, counselor," the Judge warned East. "Don't push it."

"But, Your Honor," East complained. "As originally drafted, the 13th Amendment contained twenty sections, but eighteen of those sections were deliberately concealed." He flailed his arms in a gesture of helplessness. "What's there to like about that?" He approached the jury box. "So you kind folks won't think I'm mean or onery, this is what I'm going to do since the witness wants to talk about that ole' number 13, I'm going to do the talking for him so the truth will get out---."

"Objection, Your Honor!" Stubbs rumbled. "The inference is that the witness has perjured himself."

"If the shoe fits---."

Judge Roman slammed his gavel down. "I find you in contempt of this Court," he bellowed, "and I order you to jail until seven o'clock this evening. Bailiff!" he shouted. He banged his gavel. "Court is dismissed until tomorrow morning."

<<<<<<<<<<<<<<<<
SOULFIRE BOOKS
<<<<<<<<<<<<<<<<

The following morning when East walked into the Court wearing the same clothes as the day before, Stubbs jumped out of his chair and raced to the Judge's bench, demanding a side-bar.

"Your Honor," Stubbs whispered, "this act of Mister East is utterly ridiculous, an apparent ploy to elicit sympathy from the jury. You do know what he is attempting here, don't you?"

"No," the Judge rasped, "please enlighten me."

"He's advertising this woe-be-gone aura. He wants the jury to believe that you somehow double-crossed him by making him stay in jail overnight instead of letting him out at seven."

"He's insane, Your Honor," East remarked lightly. "I just decided to do something different this morning."

"And you couldn't come up with anything better than wearing a rumpled suit and foregoing a shave?"

"What can I say, Your Honor. Tough trials reduce your creative juices."

"I say, if you don't mind, Judge Roman, that we take a delay and send Mister East home so he can regroup."

"To your places, gentlemen," Judge Roman smirked. "Don't push your luck today, East."

Without delay, East walked to the jury box. "Have you ever eaten any dog food?"

Both Stubbs and Judge Roman froze, wondering just how far East was willing to push it this morning, but neither knew what to expect. They waited.

"Where was I exactly before I had to take my little vacation yesterday?"

"The 13th Amendment." It was the Judge who spoke.

"This is not your mother's nursery rhyme," East commented sadly, "and in case it gets a little ugly, I have some Kleenex in my briefcase."

"Move on, Counselor."

"Once upon a time in 1779, perpetual slavery began legally, and unfortunately for black folks, it went on and on….and on until the 13th Amendment, but a funny thing happened to the paper it was written on. Some racist bastard---."

Stubbs yelled an objection about the use of profanity which was sustained. Judge Roman waved his gavel at East menacingly, but East seemed too far out on a limb to care.

"If I let you speak," he inquired of the witness, "do you promise not to lie?"

"Your Honor," Stubbs rasped in genuine exasperation, "Counselor has no authority to extract a promise. The witness has already been sworn in."

East appeared hurt. "B-but that was between him and the Court. This is between me and him."

"It doesn't work like that, Counsel, and you know it," Stubbs scoffed. "You don't have that right."

East faced Judge Roman. "Your Honor," he blurted, "you mean that even though this witness is under my control, I don't have the right---."

"That's right, East," Stubbs interjected harshly.

East rubbed his chin. "Isn't that sorta like the federal government trying to exercise a right over a State citizen." He grinned slyly. "I see that control does not confer any rights, right guys?"

Stubbs slumped back into his chair. He knew when he had been had. Still, he silently cursed East.

Knowing that to gloat would do nothing to further his designs, East turned less combative. "Tell us about the three elements of the 13th Amendment. What were they?"

"Emancipation. Nationalization. Compensation."

"Very good. Everyone knows about the emancipation part, so tell us, if you would, about the compensation element which, by the way, was one of the concealed sections."

The witness sighed. "The amount of money was not to exceed one hundred dollars, and the land to be allotted was known as the 36' 30."

East shook his fist at the witness. "Great goodness, man. Who understands that bull,,,,er, junk. In regular people talk, you mean the Great Interior region which was largely unsettled and unexplored, don't you?"

"Yes, that is right."

"But it never happened. Why?"

The witness looked at Stubbs for help, but the black lawyer threw up his hands in despair.

"What, is Counselor Stubbs holding your cue cards or something?"

"No."

"Then, I say, start talking. What's up?"

"There were opponents---."

"*Opponents?*" East arched his eyebrows. "Do tell."

"They wanted the compensation package deleted, but when it was presented, it passed the House and the Senate."

"Was it ratified? When?"

"1865. November 18th."

"Any more drama or did the opponents let it go?"

"Not hardly. Since they were unable to defeat the compensation package, they argued that Lincoln had not signed the resolution which would have made it invalid, but an investigation proved that Lincoln had signed off on the bill on the first of February, two and a half months before he was assassinated."

"So, was it valid?"

"Yes."

"But why didn't the land get distributed?"

"As you mentioned, this was one of the sections of the 13th Amendment that was concealed."

"I'm genuinely distraught, but this is business so we have no time for tears. Let's talk about the Nationalization element." East addressed the jury. "Talk about sad." He turned back to the witness. "*Speak!*" he commanded in a gruff tone.

"*Objection*! He's badgering the witness."

"Overruled.'

"The nationalization element," the witness whispered in a tone of defeat, "called for a general registration of the former slaves so they could proclaim a nationality."

"And this was designed so that the blacks wouldn't have to have citizenship imposed upon them. They could have just as easily chosen to become nationals of Ghana, Morocco, and any other African nation, correct?"

"Yes."

"What happened with the registration?"

"It never happened," the witness snorted. "The opponents bribed the black man authorized to conduct the General Registration."

"Bribed? I find that hard to believe. As a black man, he had to know how vital this registration was. Let me ask you something. This black man, was he deaf, dumb…blind?"

"No," the witness sighed. "He was quite literate. He was also very prominent and well-known."

"But susceptible to a bribe?"

"Evidently."

"My God, man," East uttered in mock horror, "just what was it that the opponents used to bribe a man who had to know just how vital his mission was? For the record, what did they give him? All the gold the earth contains?"

"No."

"Diamonds?"

"No."

"Silver, then?"

"No."

"All the tea in China, perhaps?"

"Again, no."

"Then what, dammit," East blurted.

"A white woman and some money."

The Court erupted with a huge gasp and a loud murmur.

"I'll be damned," East shrieked.

Judge Roman banged his gavel loudly. "Order! Order in the Court!"

Once calm was restored, East stood alone in the well of the Courtroom as if he was wondering what had happened. He paused longer than necessary, pretending he needed the extra time to recover.

"So, what you're telling this Court is that the Great Registration never started?"

"Exactly."

"Do you know what that tells me?" East grabbed his head like his brain was bleeding. "The Negro never claimed a nationality, the 13th Amendment never naturalized him, and the 14th Amendment broke the law by forcing natural citizenship upon him." He shook his head. "I know I may go back to jail for saying this, but wasn't that a bitch!"

The Court exploded in a noisy uproar.

SIX

"Dammit, East," Gulliver gushed, "you're a fucking wrecking ball. In a couple of more days, damn if you won't have pumped all the blood out of Stubbs' black ass. Any way you look at it, we have the upper hand." He slapped East on the shoulder happily. "This 14th Amendment issue is the greatest strategy of all time. Thanks, old buddy." The men embraced warmly. "Thanks for the privilege of knowing the empire is safe again." Gulliver poured drinks. "You don't know, can't even begin to imagine what this means to me, East. You've single-handedly saved the company my father built from scratch. The old man poured his whole life into QuickSilver, and I'd die before I let someone fuck with it."

"It's not quite over yet," East reminded Gulliver, "and it would be foolish to count Maurice Stubbs out. He knows how to make opportunities out----."

"Of what, thin air? You're not giving him shit , East. Not only that, but he recognizes it. Now, he may not submit, but he knows that ultimately he'll lose."

East toasted. "Here's to happy endings."

Gulliver tossed back the drink and smiled. "Yes, but to happy endings with supplements."

"Supplements?"

"Beyond your wildest imagination, my boy." Gulliver refilled their glasses. "In the business world, a threat with muscles can be your most important commodity, and when used right, nothing is hotter." Gulliver's grin grew evil and sinister. "I've kept a sharp eye out on everything that's been going on, and it's not just QuickSilver we're saving. Hell, we're rescuing the whole of corporate America, and now it's about time they paid us our respect."

"What kind of purge do you have in mind?" East teased.

"No purges this time," Gulliver offered by way of a correction. "What I have planned is more of a merger."

"Merger? Hmm."

"And in the face of what we---me and you, old buddy---have done, the industry better lick our asses and like it."

"What the hell are you talking about?" East said half-jokingly. "What I'm getting is that you are getting ready to threaten someone."

Gulliver smiled. "What I'm about to do amounts to the biggest corporate takeover in the history of the world."

"W-hat or who are you getting ready to take over?"

"Everyone."

"Everyone?"

"Yep. Everyone in corporate America. For the privilege of saving their hides from the darkies, they are going to have to pay out of their noses. We're going to squeeze these bastards for a sizeable chunk of their action, minority ownership, seats on the board of their companies, the whole nine yards."

East gasped. "You don't mean---?"

Gulliver nodded. "That's right, I'm getting ready to dismantle the old corporate culture. Me and you will impact everything that is produced in this country. Every computer that gets made, every car, every morsel of food.....every rubber band. Every fucking thing will bear our stamp of approval. Everything." Gulliver grinned fiendishly. "You didn't think the bastards were going to get a free ride, did you?"

"I-I hadn't considered anything other than the case. I didn't think in terms of redefining the marketplace." East scratched his head. "They will owe us, though."

"Big fucking time, Gulliver blurted. "QuickSilver will lead the pack. Everyone must bow down to us. And why not, they will owe us everything."

"Still," East pontificated, "that's a tall order."

"Not if we play our cards right."

"What's the deal?"

"Next week on the first, I intend to hold a summit, and invite all the fuckers in, and show them what's going on. I won't pull any punches. I want them to be utterly convinced---and scared shitless---and they will be once they bury their noses in all the evidence I've got. Then I'll invite them over to the trial and then I'll tell the assholes that if they don't bite the bullet, I'll have you take a dive."

"You mean, throw the trial?"

"Exactly." Gulliver refilled the whiskey glasses. "Some threat, huh?"

The enormity of what Gulliver planned left East speechless, but he had to admit that the threat of losing everything would be a strong enough persuader that most of the bosses wouldn't fight back. It was especially hard to imagine, but East knew there would be a few companies who would huddle their CFOs, their general counsels, and their VPs of strategy, and fight to remain independent; however eventually they would cave in. Gulliver's hand would be too strong.

"Man, this is something," East croaked.

"It's a cinch. None of them will play hard ball once they realize their quality of life is up for grabs. Name one screwball who'd want to sacrifice his caviar and champagne or his fancy Lear jet." Gulliver smirked. "Without us, those things and all that comes with it will be lost. With no exceptions, once they get the picture, they'll be praying you prevail in Court."

"I guess you're right, but how will this new corporate order be pieced together?"

"QuickSilver at the top. It's that simple."

"It's intriguing."

"Fuck intrigue. Think lucrative. Once I gather all the majors which includes every one of the Fortune 500---."

"Whew!"

"You can say that again. I'm not bullshitting. I'm kicking ass and taking names, and this is the deal. All 500 of the companies must restructure so that we own 49% of the stock in each individual company. Also every one of the companies will become a functioning subsidiary of QuickSilver."

"Whew!"

Gulliver laughed. "Hot shit, huh?"

"Mind-boggling."

"Everything will be incorporated under the QuickSilver logo. We'll be the parent company, but they'll be free to conduct business as before, however QuickSilver will reserve the right to detail goals, and we'll have the enforcement power to pressure any slackers should the need arise."

East could tell Gulliver was proud of himself. He was getting ready to usher in a new way of doing business: his way. And if this little pep rally was any indication of what the 'new breakthrough' would represent, then he had just inherited a billion dollar baby. At once, East broke out in an almost uncontrollable spasm of giddy laughter. "Boy," he uttered joyfully, "is life great or what?"

SOULFIRE BOOKS

Meanwhile.

When trial resumed on Monday, the last day of the month, Stubbs had to talk himself into not flipping his wig, and that nearly didn't work. He sat in total stone-faced horror as Judge Roman swore in another alternate juror. He sighed with profound resignation as he watched the jury box being reinvented, and with this recognition came the desire to reach over and to choke the shit out of East.

Now, more than not, Stubbs began to lose the trickle of hope he once had about this trial being as fair as circumstances would allow. Now, thanks to the devious schemes of the Merchant family, it was, suddenly, either boom-or-bust. There were no other options. All his perquisites were gone.

"Your Honor," Stubbs groaned miserably, "may I humbly request a recess?"

SOULFIRE BOOKS

The question was not if the witness would crack---but when. East had been like a legal sorcerer, and his cross-examinations had been brilliant. With skillful pokes, he had magically scaled back so much weight off the prosecutor's case that the prosecutor himself seemed ready to abandon ship.

With his characteristic bullying, East seemed to viscerally delight in knowing how precariously close he was to inducing a massive coronary on the witness who was already trembling and faint.

Stubbs felt obligated to do something to halt the carnage, but all he could do was to object, and to a man as brutally precise as East, such a standard, prepackaged response meant nothing.

Still…

"Objection!"

"For what?" East shouted. "I have every right to pursue this line of questioning since it was the witness who tendered the information on the 15th Amendment. I'm just making him wallow in his own vomit."

"Counselor!" the Judge yelled. "Watch your language. Overruled."

East's eyes glinted as he went back to the attack. "Is it or is it not true that the 15th Amendment is commonly known as one of the three dead badges of the law?"

"Yes,"

"The other two being the 13th and 14th?"

"Yes."

"Thanks for the clarification, but now let's take a close look at the infamy of the 15th Amendment, shall we. First off, the 15th is about voting, isn't it?"

"That's true."

"Oh yes, before I forget, let me ask you if, under the Constitution, does the United States have any voters of its own?"

"No."

"And would that be because only the State citizens could vote?"

"Yes."

"So, then isn't it true that the 15th Amendment did nothing more than make it discriminatory to exempt any individual from voting due to race, color, or previous condition of servitude?'

"Yes." The witness was weary.

"Then that can only mean that the right to vote came from the States while the right of exception from the prohibited discrimination comes from the United States. That also means that only the right of State citizens to vote is constitutionally protected, right?"

"Yes, once again."

East walked deliberately slow and stood in front of the lone, black juror. Now,   tell me once more. Only citizens of a State are legitimately eligible to vote, right?"

"That is correct, sir."

"Isn't it also correct that only legitimate voters can sit on a jury panel?"

Stubbs objected with so much vigor that it startled the Judge. Stubbs saw where East was going, recognized what he was getting at, and he had to stop him.

"Overruled."

East shot Stubbs a sinister glare before returning his attention back to the witness. "So," he rasped, "if a person is not a legitimate citizen of a State, he can't vote, can he?"

"No."

"Well, if that same person is not a legitimate State citizen with no legitimate voting power, can he legally sit on a jury?"

"No sir, not legally. Not in the US."

East stared at the black juror. "We must be on the damned moon, then." He quickly looked at Judge Roman, smiling politely. "I have no further questions, Your Honor."

SOULFIRE BOOKS

Less than three hours after Court had adjourned for the evening, Congressman Peterson felt silly trying to console Stubbs while at the same time attempting to convince himself that all was not lost when everyone in the hotel room knew the prosecution was scrambling to stay alive. The mere idea of a comeback was foolish thinking, and no one was quite sure where to refocus their energy since East had left them with so little to build on. The bottom line was that the handwriting was beginning to appear on the wall, and everyone knew what it would say: ***BETTER LUCK NEXT TIME!*** But there would be no next time. No matter how warped the verdict might turn out to be, it would pretty much signal the total destruction of black America. In an ideal world, there would be a second chance as the case would round through the appeal process, but as misguided as the notion seemed now, both sides had eagerly agreed to abandon this option. How remarkably silly.

The case was running on schedule, even if the results he had hoped for were not. Unfortunately, there were no affirmations or meditations that could be used to snap things back to normal again because in essence, there would never be such a thing as normal ever again. Suddenly, crying seemed the thing to do. Real tears.

On one side of the room, Cinque stood motionless for a while longer, listening to Stubbs weakly outline what he would do now that the prosecution had rested its case, but when he got tired of trying to look tough in the face of apparent defeat, he rushed to the phone."

"*Get guns!*" he yelled into the receiver. "*Get guns!*"

Without thinking, the Congressman darted over to depress the button, disconnecting the call, "Are you crazy?"

"No," Cinque spat, "but you are if you think I'm going to sit around and get squashed like a bug." He slapped Peterson's hand off the phone. "Dying like a dog in the streets ain't a part of my history."

"It's not over, Cinque. Don't give up, please."

"Brotha," Cinque responded, his voice choked, "winning now has just become unthinkable."

Stubbs knew he needed to say something to defend their position but, contrary to that belief, he had nothing to say. They'd all been in the courtroom and most of them had personally observed the legal carnage East had brought down on him, so it wasn't like they were unaware of the ass-kicking he was getting.

Sitting forlornly in an oversized chair, Jamal struggled to remain composed, yet inwardly he wondered if this wasn't the right time for the other door to be opening because one door damned sure had closed.

Cinque spoke. "What sense does it make to go on talking about taking advantage of a situation that is beyond repair? We're busted, man, and if the rest of you brothas want to wave it off, hoping to find the proverbial silver lining, then just don't expect me to play along." He walked to where a dejected Stubbs sat, perched on the edge of a chair. "Look, I'm not coming down on the brotha. He did his thing, but he lost every chance we had to battle back. It's sad, but I don't see no way he can reduce the chances of failure. It's just that bad, and I was thinking that it was about time we faced reality."

"You want to fight, right?"

"Damn right, Jomo. They're going to kill us."

Sensing an argument, Jamal found his voice. "Mister Stubbs, I'm very interested in hearing your thoughts about the rest of the trial"

Stubbs knew his eyes looked vacant, and he also understood that the thunder in his voice had depreciated considerably, and he couldn't even guess the number of times he had prayed that no one would ask him that question. It posed too many limitations. "Don't count me out," he said softly.

SEVEN

October arrived awash in a contaminated flux. It seemed more plastic than September had been, digitally more dangerous where every eight out of ten minutes felt universally sinister. Somehow the morning gave off the lurid impression that it was inventing and then reinventing itself as it went along, embodying itself around the premise that it was out to either refine or to redefine everyone's deepest fears.

Court was already underway in Bolivar County, and now it was East who had the task of shepherding his witnesses through the blistering cross-examination of the adversary.

East fully expected Stubbs to meddle as much as possible with untimely objections, but such a ruse was too remote to be much of a miracle. The die was cast, and it was all over except the shouting---and the shooting. East forced the ugly images away, and returned to his witness. "Tell us more."

"These principles have been maintained by our Constitution, but they have not always been adopted by the courts."

"And why is that, you think?"

"Professor Wheeler winced. "Convenience, perhaps. To admit such things would present prima facie evidence that the character of the National government was in direct opposition to any of the claims it spoke so highly of."

"Elaborate on that, will you?"

Wheeler shrugged. "The native Americans made it as plain as it ever will be when they said that the white man spoke with forked tongue. That offered proof to them that there was a double standard, meaning that what the white man's government said on paper did not necessarily reflect what was in his heart."

"All in all, then, what you're saying is that many of the principles we have regarded as beyond reproach are, and have always been, open to question. Is that what you're trying to establish?"

"I need not establish anything," Wheeler huffed. "The evidence calls forth its own proof."

"Just the same, Professor Wheeler, the Court requires us to hear you on the matter. We, laymen, are not sufficiently equipped with your legal insight." East smiled. "Just how long have you been a Professor of law?"

"Thirty-five years."

"I thought that was what you had said earlier, but I had to be sure. Thanks for your patience, but let's go back to my earlier question. Just what do you mean?"

"The whole doctrine of constitutional amendments beyond the original ten is not strengthened by law as the Bill of Rights is the only authentic certificate that is legally binding. The principles laid down therein are irrevocable, expressly recognized by all courts."

"And the attachments thereafter?"

"They are legally fraudulent."

"Let's be specific. What about the 14th Amendment?"

Wheeler gestured absently with his hands. "The 14th is patently untrue as to the exercise of its function."

"Is that as bad as it sounds? Explain for the Court."

"It has been found that the provisions of law enumerated in the 14th Amendment had been deemed insufficient to extend citizenship to the newly freed slaves. Since they were never domiciles of any State, documentary evidence suggests that the most the 14th Amendment could have done was to enact a transfer of property."

"A property transfer?"

"Yes. The slaves as property were merely transferred from regional ownership to governmental ownership."

"Was that a good deal?"

Wheeler shrugged. "When blacks became national citizens, the title of ownership was as complete as required by law, but relative to actual citizenship rights, it invested the blacks with nothing. In truth, the blacks had just been sold again, accompanied this time by delivery to the federal government as a legal fiction."

East strutted a bit. "Is it thereby clear, on the point you just mentioned, that if a Negro, black, or African-American person, in any instance, tried to pursue recourse in a court of law, his demand could not be satisfied since there is proof that he has no citizenship rights?"

"Absolutely. Statelessness---?"

"Hold it," East interrupted. "Are you telling the Court that black people are,,,Stateless. Is that, is that your position?"

"The position is not mine, but the government's. Black people, well, they are decreed as stateless, and this condition has placed them outside the influence of both executive and judicial power."

"Why?"

"Because," Wheeler sighed, shaking his head. "It's unfortunate, but not only is the black man exempted from the laws of this nation, but international law also."

"What, if anything, does international law decree?"

Wheeler closed his eyes tightly for a second, then reopened them slowly. "International law is such and I quote: *'As far as the law of nations is concerned, a Stateless person does not possess any nationality, enjoys in general, no protection whatsoever and if he is aggrieved by a State has no means of redress'*." Wheeler clasped his eyes shut again. "I'm sorry." His eyes popped open. "The government of the US has no right to aid the black race in the recovery of their rights since, by law, they possess none."

"Stay with me now," East pleaded. "This is nothing personal and no one is going to accuse you of being racist simply because you quote the law, but it is important to this Court that the truth be heard. With that in mind, I ask you, Professor Wheeler, if or not, the Constitution conferred upon the government the power to either establish or to legalize rights for blacks?"

"Notwithstanding State citizenship, both the State and national governments were obliged to recognize that the black man had no rights, no matter how repugnant the decision was."

"Even though they appear as free men?"

"The circumstances that pronounced them free left no instructions as to their citizenship."

"But they were free."

"Yes, they were, but just like one of their own, Sojourner Truth said…..'they were free to roam…free to be hungry…free to die.'"

A huge droning murmur arose in the Court, but before it reached fever pitch and Judge Roman had to contain it, the noise abated.

East, pleased with the reaction, grinned wolfishly. "Your Honor, I have no further questions."

The following week.

The buzzards were no longer hovering over his head, and now that Stubbs had pulled the trigger on his latest strategy, he reentered the fray with a super-charged vigor. He had come roaring back just when everyone had believed he was down for the count, and now here he was, embarrassing the defense. Not only was East's case hanging in the balance, it was tottering, and the entire Court noticed that the momentum had suddenly shifted.

It rejuvenated Stubbs to notice the sparkle back in the eyes of Congressman Peterson and his other supporters who no longer clung to the desperate prospect of becoming sore losers. Life, for them, once more had relevance. Sure, a case could rise or fall for no apparent reason given the whiplash-like push and pull dynamics of courtroom drama, but currently what Stubbs was doing was nothing more than sitting squarely in the middle of the road, popping up every now and then to score a big psychological punch, and then blocking East dramatically when the defense tried to recover. It wasn't visually stunning, but it was far from shabby. He glared at East spitefully. *There would be no bargains today, buddy.*

After recess, Stubbs welcomed the witness back to the Terror-Dome. "That's pretty interesting, Professor McKinley, but I find quite a bit of constitutional turbulence in your argument. For instance, there is another species of rights that no one has cared to discuss, and it sorta bugs me, and I feel that since no one has done it, I deputize you to set the record straight. Now, we all know that rights have a kissing cousin." Stubbs smiled for the jury as if they were paparazzi out to snap his photo, but after a second, he returned to the witness. "Isn't it true that there are jurisdictional rights?"

"Yes sir."

"Tell us what that means exactly."

"Just that rights can be jurisdictionally defined."

"Are jurisdictional rights useless?"

"They are just as enforceable as inherent ones."

"My preliminary question is this, Professor McKinley. Isn't it true that in order for the newly freed slave to be unprejudiced by his lack of inherent rights, he was endowed with jurisdictional ones?"

"That is correct."

"And you just said a moment ago that jurisdictional rights were as protected as inherent ones, right?"

"I did."

"So, that means that black people's jurisdictional rights entitled them to basically the same protections as white people derived from their inherent rights?"

"Yes, I would imagine so."

"So, let me ask this. The presumption of jurisdictional rights for blacks retains for them a domicile of origin in whatever State they choose to reside regardless of whether or not they were naturalized or nationalized there, isn't that absolutely correct, Professor?"

"Yes."

"That being so, a *nationalized* black would enjoy all the privileges and immunities as would a *naturalized* white, right?"

"Right."

"I see," Stubbs smiled. "Wouldn't it be incumbent upon the State of domicile of a naturalized white to seek an indictment against an accused party in the event the naturalized person was murdered?"

Professor McKinley shrugged. "Of course, yes."

"But why is what I'm asking," Stubbs prodded.

"Why?" the Professor scowled "is because it's the law, that's why."

"And naturalized whites and nationalized blacks have the same rights?"

"They do, sir."

"Would it be incumbent upon the State of domicile of a nationalized black to seek an indictment against an accused party in the event the nationalized person was murdered?"

"Yes sir," the Professor retorted testily.

"But why is what I'm asking."

The scowl on the Professor's face deepened. "Because it's the damned law."

<<<<<<<<<<<<<<<<
SOULFIRE BOOKS
<<<<<<<<<<<<<<<<<

Herold Pictet had never heard anything like this is his complete life, and nothing had ever upset him more. And yes, he would act. At once.

Every so often he could be moved to righteous indignation, and on those occasions when he was, he gave little or no quarter, and could be quite dangerous. That was a wrinkle most people never saw reflected in his naked character, but it was there nonetheless, but what was now important was the test-within-the-test. Had he loved Bill enough to avenge his death? To say that he had loved Bill with all his heart would not be far off the mark, and that would be only an index of what he knew Bill felt for him. They had been two individuals overwhelmingly in love with each other.

Herold offered himself a half-dozen reasons why he should inevitably punish those responsible for his lover's death, and all of them made too much sense to ignore, so he polled himself one final time, and then made a phone call.

The man Herold contacted was one he would, under normal circumstances, avoid like the Ebola plague, but this was not normal, so he shrank his repulsion and devised a formula that would satisfy the debt the man owed him.

Herold grimaced, gritting his teeth. Terrorism was such a deplorable occupation, but even those who engaged in it had need of a reliable source with a knack for book-keeping tactics that could squeeze a dollar out of an eagle's ass, and then make it disappear.

Herold Pictet was such a man. He could hide money and anyone who tried to hunt for it would find themselves on a financial roller-coaster going nowhere, and this is why Ibrahim Kunduz valued him so much.

"As-Salaam-Alaikum, Brother Herold. This must be momentous. You never call."

"I-I need a favor."

"Ask it, my friend."

"I---."

"Ask it, and it is yours."

"I-I need some martyrs."

Ibrahim Kunduz grunted in amusement. "And I thought you wanted something. No sooner said than done."

EIGHT

The atmosphere was not sunny, but Gulliver was by no means unnerved by the tension in the room which radiated with the very real vibe of impending doom; the tension both symphonic and catastrophic.

Exaggeration? No. That's exactly how it felt to all the chairmen and CEOs of the celebrated top Fortune 500 companies who had gathered at the Marriott. All were cranky, clearly insensitive to the rotten idea of being called out on a moment's notice to a meeting that already seemed like an out-of-body experience. Some others were tragically unsentimental and would bear a lifelong grudge if the trajectory of this clandestine meeting failed to live up to its billing as "TOP PRIORITY". One or two of the others were men who shared a passion for large-scale intrigue, and simply loved being in on anything at the ground floor. They were the only ones in the cavernous auditorium that appeared animated. Earlier, Gulliver had described himself as Superman, and the perception had not dimmed when he stepped to the podium to address the audience. Despite dismissing all of his pretenses and shedding his 'hired gun' mentality, he was still ready to lay waste to everything these corporate moguls believed in. Some would shout that he was going too far, and he couldn't imagine not being ceremonially branded as a greedy opportunist eager to gobble up other companies' goodies, but fuck 'em, Gulliver thought.

"Gentlemen," he began, "this, basically is a horror story."

Almost as soon as he had started talking, he was finished, but notwithstanding the brevity, none misinterpreted the monstrous implications and consequences of what had been said, Yet it all came down to this: could East win? The mere prospect of awakening in an America without their corporates perks was a soulless proposition none of them could accept.

"I'm not a racketeer," Gulliver confessed, "but if I'm going to carry the load by helping you preserve your power and influence, then hell yeah, I'm attaching a fee."

"But it's extortion," the rep from General Motors shouted.

"Yeah, but try the alternative," Gulliver spat back.

Personnel from Tyco International stood and spoke. "No one man, meaning you, Mister Merchant, should be vested with the power of Caesar. It is unfathomable that QuickSilver Properties should be elevated to the one bright, shining monopoly in this country."

"Either that or you piss away everything. Look" Gulliver said calmly, "I'm not here to argue with you guys or to debate the pros and cons of my proposal. I'm telling you what my financial quote is, and that's a fair take. End of story."

"Excuse me. Excuse me, Mister Merchant." It was a female CEO. "This is extraordinary."

"And."

"You don't have to be so rude, do you?"

"Look, Miss," Gulliver announced, "this is not the Oprah show on breast implants. Grow up."

"May you burn in hell for this."

"Next!" Gulliver snapped dismissively.

Time Warner wanted to know if Gulliver understood that such a massive re-structuring of these companies could collapse many of them. "49%, Mister Merchant. Doesn't that smack of greed?"

Gulliver laughed derisively. "Greed? When many of you plundered banks, and, in some instances, foreign countries, there was no concern if the economy was distressed or not, so keep your shirts on. QuickSilver will offer a bailout---."

The room erupted in shouts and cries of 'Robber Baron', and 'Death to QuickSilver', but when the ruckus threatened to explode into violence, security quickly dispelled the budding disturbance. The few who chose to continue yelling were roughly escorted from the meeting.

Once peace was restored, Gulliver returned to the podium. "What a bunch of eccentrics," he joked.

"Get on with it, you bloodsucker," someone hollered from the back of the auditorium, "Don't prolong the agony."

Gulliver's face hardened. "Anyone who doesn't want to credit me with saving their corporate asses can get up and leave right this instant."

"*No one moved.*

"Anyone who doesn't mind losing their companies are free to exit the premises."

No one moved.

"Anyone who doesn't want to transfer 49% of their company stock to QuickSilver Properties can also get the hell out. Now!"

Not a soul moved.

"*Then I am Caesar!*" Gulliver exclaimed triumphantly.

SOULFIRE BOOKS

The energy inside the Courtroom crackled.

This was the last day of testimony and both lawyers fought for advantage, desperately looking for a last-round knockout. Winning was definitely a high priority, and both Stubbs and East slipped in a slew of punches before the mid-morning recess.

SOULFIRE BOOKS

Stubbs looked at Peterson questioningly. "What do you think?"

"You've been excellent over the last ten days, and it's my honest opinion that we can win this."

Stubbs hugged Peterson tightly. "Thanks I needed to hear that."

"You've hit him in all the right places at all the right times," Jamal added. "You've practically milked his case. I feel good about the way things are going."

With a tear in his eyes, Stubbs hugged the young man, "You guys have me pumped up." He held out a hand to Cinque. "And your feelings?"

Cinque hesitated, then gripped the extended hand. "You're kicking that cracker's ass, man. Right on!"

"You guys go on back in." Stubbs looked at his watch. "I need a few minutes to mobilize mentally. I need to finish strong."

SOULFIRE BOOKS

Similarly, East struggled not to be distracted.

"How do you evaluate it?" he quizzed his assistant.

Without a trace of indecision, the man responded. "You've got it in the bag. The guy should call it quits right now and concede. Don't think I'm slighting the bastard because the man, wow, he can dance, but my hat is off to you." The assistant grinned, extending his hand. "You're the fucking best in the whole world."

East savored the compliment because he also felt he had handled the case exceptionally well, and reckoned that he'd both outfoxed and outboxed Stubbs, but man, what a legal rendezvous!

Though he had never seriously considered he would lose, he also never figured that Stubbs would still be this close in his rearview mirror at this stage in the trial, but no matter. He always saved the best for last.

SOULFIRE BOOKS

The prediction proved true enough. Now that the wild, legal, merry-go-round ride had almost ground to a halt, the courtroom spectators, acting on principle, defined where there stood, and the division was as clear as the Mason-Dixon line.

By the time the defense had called its last witness, the spectators were taking things much more personal, and no one was willing to straddle the fence. Everyone wanted to weigh in.

The jury, however, was less casual about their choices, and none of them seemed eager to compromise their official obligation to remain stoic, but still the nervousness and wariness announced that they were ready to get out of the breach, and into the jury room where they could slug it out. They were ready to get the pent-up emotions out of their system and to cleanse themselves, knowing that the real work lie in becoming functional again. For over a month, they had served as robots courted by a pair of flamboyant lawyers who hoped to be the go-to-player when the verdict was returned, elevating one and condemning the other.

The arguments on both sides had been well-crafted and well-greased by supporting facts and testimony, and there had indeed been magic. It had been exquisitely spectacular, a wonderfully staged legal battle, but this evening it would end, except for the verdict of the jury which would ultimately scar American politics.

So be it!

At around one thirty pm, East stood in the well of the courtroom in a notorious silence as if the very nature of what he said next would extend some great favor upon all of mankind. The people prayed that he would continue with his witness, but since they lacked the power or force to compel him to speak, they themselves remained mute, stewing in the total silence.

When trial had first started in September, East had appeared so much younger. Now, it looked almost as if he had integrated his next five birthdays into one, and then had one helluva party to celebrate the accomplishment, but he was still a great believer in himself, and being very fond of this larger-than life belief, he resonated with authority.

Migrating in his mind to the margins of wherever it was he was concentrating on, he mumbled something, an intimately personal reminder to either do or not do some great perplexing thing, and lastly he smiled.

"Now, Professor, without offense, I implore you to answer if or not the 14th Amendment was devised so as to assume jurisdiction over the blacks?"

"Objection!" Stubbs shouted. "Calls for speculation on witness's behalf since he has no way of knowing what was assumed."

East smiled. "It was my purpose, Your Honor, to get a report---."

"But a speculative report, at best."

"Not hardly, since the witness as a law professor is part of a small group which has studied the Constitution."

"Still," Stubbs argued, "even assiduous study can conclude with a false representation of what---."

"Your Honor," East declared emphatically, "counsel is intending to deny the Court of expert testimony."

"I intend nothing of the sort." Stubbs jumped to his feet. "I just don't want personal conjecture inserted into the record, that's all."

"Is it, counsel?" East snarled.

"I want to see justice served, if that is what you imply."

"In that case, you should sit down and let me finish my examination." East beckoned to the Judge. "Your Honor, would you direct counsel to take his seat. He is making a spectacle of these solemn proceedings. If---."

"You're the one---."

Judge Roman banged the gavel. *"Gentlemen!"*

Both men pointed accusingly at the other like two schoolboys squabbling over a broken pencil. Their childish antics elicited spasms of giggles throughout the courtroom.

"As strange as it seems, "I'm not going to tolerate any last minute temper tantrums from either of you. Is that clear?"

"Your Honor," Stubbs pleaded, "I apologize to the Court if it somehow feels I was purposely disruptive, but the objection was reasonable, and in no way intended as a means of evading the scrutiny---.

"But that's exactly what it conveyed, Your Honor," East countered. "If there was a basis for the objection, counsel could have pressed the issue under the scrutiny of cross."

"Overruled."

"Thank you, Your Honor."

Stubbs sat down defiantly.

"Answer the question," Judge Roman directed the witness.

"Between the government and the slave-holding States, the 14th Amendment was more of a permit that settled the question of ownership of the blacks. Blacks were never actually put on board the 14th Amendment as citizens, but as legal property of the government. It was all a fraud, this citizen--."

"Objection, Your Honor!" Stubbs shouted. "Witness has no legitimate way, despite what he claims to know, to have any real idea what the framers of the 14th Amendment had in mind when they crafted the legislation. Any answer would be pure speculation, Your Honor."

East flung his hands about in exasperation. "It we were to consign the tag of speculation to every piece of evidence, whether scientific, legal, or otherwise, then we would still be shitting in the woods---."

"Counselor!" Judge Roman roared.

"I'm sorry, Your Honor," East contended, "but not one of us today had any idea what Mister Crapper, the man who invented the commode, had in mind when he taught us to flush our----."

The Judge banged his gavel. "I'm warning you, Counselor."

The Court giggled aloud.

"All we know is that the contraption won't work if we overload it, and that's---."

"What's the point of all this colorful bathroom humor, Your Honor. It's disgusting to say the least."

"I'm just showing that the 14th Amendment won't work if you overload it with---

"With what, counselor?" Stubbs stood and faced East. "Are you getting ready to liken black people to shit?"

"Order! Order in the Court!" the Judge yelled when the courtroom erupted in wild shrieks and chatter, and when the noise did finally ebb, he called for a sidebar conference, then adjourned for a ten minute recess.

<<<<<<<<<<<<<<<<
SOULFIRE BOOKS
<<<<<<<<<<<<<<<<<

This was personal. By now, both lawyers nurtured a private hatred for each other, and over-appreciated the fact that they were, for the survival of their respective race, the keeper of the flame. Both knew what winning meant, and both knew there would be no consolation prize, no second place. It was all or nothing, and neither man could bring himself to be timid in the face of the agenda they now encountered.

"I am aware that this is a hotly contested issue," the Judge cautioned, "but I'll make no provisions in this courtroom for either of you to overstep the boundaries of propriety, so I am issuing this warning early enough for you to be adequately forewarned. I want both of you to shake with the dread of what I'm do if either of you forget your place. Am I clear?"

"Yes." This from East.

Stubbs simply nodded his head.

Satisfied, the Judge ordered East back to his direct examination of Professor Graham.

"Are you familiar, Professor, with the definition of citizenship as originally given in Black's Law Dictionary?"

"I am, sir."

"Who, by that definition, are citizens?"

"White Americans, sir."

"And it said that in Black's?"

"Yes, very emphatically."

"I wonder if Black's Law Dictionary had anything to say expressly about blacks. You wouldn't, by any chance, just happen to know, would you?"

"Accordingly, sir, they---the blacks---were specifically defined as non-citizens."

"And Black's said that about blacks?"

"Yes."

"That's critical," East mused. "I can hardly believe my ears. You must know that Black's---."

"Objection, You Honor. Counselor is trying to lead the jury to believe that Black's Law Dictionary is the Holy Bible. I object to the inference."

"Overruled. Move on."

"Professor Graham, it appears that due to the 14th Amendment, the black race will try to present themselves as valid, bonafide US citizens. Is that possible?"

"They---the blacks---would have to look far beyond the 14th Amendment for their citizenship rights."

"The Constitution, then?"

"Not there."

"Where, then, God?"

"*Objection!*" Stubbs was on his feet. "Witness cannot speak for God. It's bad enough he's sitting up there like he's some clairvoyant, knowing all these things, but Your Honor, don't tell me that counsel is now getting ready to pass him off as a confidant of God Almighty. Come on now."

"It was a good faith question, Your Honor, as counsel is aware. After all, such a thing as God-given rights are recognized in this country."

"Let white folks tell it."

"And black folk deny it."

"You're a hypocrite, East."

"And you're a fool."

"Counselors!" Judge Roman screamed. "To my chambers. *Now!*"

SOULFIRE BOOKS

"You want a piece of me, white boy? Think you can handle that?"

"And more." East was angry.

Judge Roman stood between the two men. "I strongly admonish the both of you to calm down because I'll censure the both of you severely if you don't get it together. "

Your Honor," East asked. "What's the problem? It's my prerogative to conduct my examination as I see fit."

"And it's my prerogative to object if the occasion arises."

"Judge Roman, it should be noted by counsel that his objections are limited to---."

"I have the right to object as many times as I please."

"Not when I'm examining a witness."

"And why not?"

"Because I'll stop you."

"Hmmph, that will be the day."

"I see," Judge Roman sighed in resignation, "that I'm going to be left with no choice but to move that the trial is complete as is. I'll instruct the jury---."

"That won't be necessary, Your Honor," Stubbs conceded.

"Counselor East?"

"Let us finish the trial, Your Honor. I don't want there to be any tears in the end."

"Okay, it's settled then," Judge Roman barked, "but I'm taking the position that if either of you stray, then I'm stepping in and putting an end to these proceedings. Do I make myself clear?"

Both attorneys nodded.

"Now go back out here so I can adjourn court for the day. Give you two more than sufficient time to cool off. Mark my words, though, gentlemen, both of you are skating on very thin ice."

SOULFIRE BOOKS

The great host in the courtroom was bitterly disappointed when Judge Roman called the session to a close. Perhaps it was for good cause, but still no one wanted to leave since it was so abundantly clear that the two lawyers were so close to punching each other. The spectators had won one more day, but how could it compare with today's fireworks? What a show!

On his way out of the courtroom, Congressman Peterson froze for a second when he noticed the four Middle-Eastern looking men. He hadn't seen them before, and immediately guessed they were friends with Cinque, but when they brushed out of the courtroom without so much as a glance at Cinque, he wondered if he was wrong. For some reason, the presence of the four men was not comforting.

"Let's go, Tiger," Peterson grinned when Stubbs caught up with him. "Boy, you looked good in there today. You kicked ass," he hooted, quickly forgetting the men.

SOULFIRE BOOKS

The fireworks started bright and early the next morning, and the entire courtroom was galvanized by the attacks and counterattacks of the lawyers. Both put on a brilliant display. Gone was the outright, personal venom of yesterday. Today, everything was done with a meticulous passion and intensity, a proselytizing flair that was a wonder to behold. Today, unlike yesterday, there were no excesses, each attorney firing damaging legal salvos from a distance, not wanting to stumble into each other's range where they would risk getting their argument crippled.

The tension was suffocating.

"So, you're saying that the provisions of the 14th Amendment were insufficient to suggest that blacks had rights under the constitution?"

"Yes, that is precisely what I'm saying."

"And since blacks had no rights under the Constitution, then it stands that Tony Rawls, like Dred Scott, had no rights that white men were bound to respect?"

"That is true, sir."

"Even murder?"

"The deceased had no rights, sir."

"There was an indictment."

"It is derelict as to its inference."

"Is that the same as saying---?"

"No good?"

East smiled. "You took the words right out of my mouth."

"Any such indictment, under those circumstances, is frivolous and has neither merit nor standing in a Court of law. It is of no effect."

East shrugged. "Then that means---?"

The witness leaned forward. "Then that means that your client, Officer Rand, is completely innocent of the murder of Tony Rawls,"

"Your Honor," East quipped assuredly. "I rest my case."

<<<<<<<<<<<<<<<
SOULFIRE BOOKS
<<<<<<<<<<<<<<<<<

The great trial was now over. Nothing more was left but the rendering of the verdict, immediately after which scores would be settled, and because relations between the two parties were strained to the utmost, it was sure that no compromises would be given. The winner would take all.

At the beginning of the deliberations, the feelings seemed to be that the prosecution was favored, but this early opinion suddenly reversed, and the defense abruptly became the jury's darling; however, much quicker than it should have, the sentiment shifted again, making a sharp turn back to the prosecution.

Then the jury was released for the night.

On October 10th, the next morning, everyone was startled when the jury requested a fresh review of the Tony Rawls indictment as well as a copy of the 14th Amendment. Later that same morning--- approximately one hour later---the jury made it known that they wished to study certain portions of the transcribed record.

At all times when the jurors were inside the courtroom, the two lawyers shed their aloofness and tried to appear as saintly as possible, each hoping to become the apple of the jury's eye. This was their last chance to take a lead role in the juror's perspective because, after this, they would be as out of sight as a ghost.

Stubbs leaned to his left in an attempt to get as close to the jury as possible. Seeing this, East took the initiative to smile brightly, his final master-stroke.

The jury departed.

NINE

On the other hand, Congressman Petersen decided to ask Cinque about the four bearded men. As far as he could judge, they didn't seem to be associated with either side of the trial, but each day since last week, they had shown up, and on the last two occasions had somehow exhibited a rabid scorn and disgust for everything in particular about the proceeding. Yet, what disturbed Peterson most was that the outcome of the trial would grant them no advantages either way, so there was nothing to justify their in-court presence. Peterson shuddered. The men gave him the creeps. They looked like terrorists.

<<<<<<<<<<<<<<<
SOULFIRE BOOKS
<<<<<<<<<<<<<<<<<

Soon after a short recess, the jury was ordered back to their deliberations, and again both Stubbs and East returned to their outsider status.

To a certain extent, both were compelled to going their own way, but a chance meeting in the hallway gave them one last opportunity to provoke the other. However, neither seized the moment.

"You're a helluva attorney," East commented sincerely. "Great going in there."

Stubbs smiled slightly. "My hat is off to you, East. You're one of the best."

East extended his hand. Stubbs reached for it, but Gulliver intervened, knocking East's outstretched hand away.

"Don't shake that nigger's hand," Gulliver snarled. "He's a dead man walking, anyway."

Peterson pushed his way through the crowd, confronting Gulliver. "You coward."

"Me? A coward?"

"That's right," Peterson repeated coldly. "You're nothing but a coward who hides behind others to do your dirty work."

"Is that what you truly believe, Congressman?"

"It is."

Gulliver rocked back and forth on the balls of his feet. "So, you think I lack balls, huh? Well, I'll tell you what---."

East and Stubbs wedged themselves between the two, hoping to keep them separated.

Gulliver laughed spitefully. "Get this, a fucking congressional comic. You're a clown, Peterson."

"And your ass is mine when this is finished, and you can find that funny if you want to, but I wouldn't advise it." Peterson balled his fists. "I owe you, you bastard. You killed my niece."

"Hopefully, I'll get credit when the rest of you darkies join her."

Jamal swung, connecting with a solid punch that sent Gulliver reeling backwards. Enraged, Gulliver unleashed a barrage of punches of his own, striking Stubbs.

Pandemonium ensued.

Rapidly informed of the melee in the hallway, Judge Roman hastily rushed from his chambers, but by the time he had arrived, security had physically separated the two warring factions.

"What the hell is going on?!" the Judge yelled at no one in particular." He glared at both Stubbs and East. "Someone is going to tell me something," he snapped. "I have half a mind to have both of you arrested." He glanced at his bailiffs as if considering the idea. "Who started it---?"

"The jury is back in," a reporter shouted over the din. "They've reached a decision."

Stubbs and East raced back inside the Courtroom to take their places. The rest of the crowd rushed in behind them, pushing, shoving; wanting good seats.

East rearranged the silk handkerchief to disguise the ragged tear in the breast pocket of his gabardine suit.

Stubbs merely hoped he looked well-organized, and prayed he wasn't bleeding from any of the many places where he'd been punched.

A few seconds later, Judge Roman regally entered the courtroom from his chambers, his face an impassive mask. He conveyed nothing, and both lawyers were glad the Judge had regained his judicial bearings, but both cast worried looks at the jury when the gavel sounded, and Court was ordered back into session. This was it, they reckoned. After all the innumerable words spoken; after all the indescribable legal footwork, the long march to a verdict was over, but suddenly neither attorney seemed to be in any great rush to find out the fate of the other.

"Have you reached a verdict?" the Judge bellowed with passion and authority.

The jury foreman stood. "We have, Your Honor."

SOULFIRE BOOKS

In the opinion of Herold Pictet, it had to end this way. Even though he had wished that he hadn't had to take a stand, he had. When they had murdered Bill, it had become virtually impossible for him not to have a hand in the whole sordid affair. They should have asked around because if they had, they would have learned that when you fucked with Herold Pictet, you paid the price.

SOULFIRE BOOKS

Congressman Petersen couldn't pretend he hadn't noticed that the four men were not sitting huddled together as usual. He saw only one, but instantly perceived it hardly unlikely that the others were absent. On a whim, Peterson craned his neck, looking over the room, spotting one, then another of the bearded men, and for no other reason except completion, he swiveled around, scanning faces until he had placed the fourth man. Turning back to listen to the Judge, it dawned on him that the men were spread out in a box-like configuration. "That's strange," he muttered to himself.

<<<<<<<<<<<<<<<<
SOULFIRE BOOKS
<<<<<<<<<<<<<<<<

It was interesting that East felt like this, and the more he thought about it, the more he realized that Judge Roman was indeed the final intercessor between the most controversial verdict in American history, and the awful consequences it would bring. East shivered involuntarily. It was inconceivable, scarcely possible, that Judge Roman could even begin to imagine the untold horror he was about to usher in upon his mere request for a verdict. At least, East was sure he had won.

SOULFIRE BOOKS

Clemency of any sort would be at total odds with everything that had gone into his case, Stubbs thought, so he'd give no quarter. This was war. The white devil needed to be checkmated, and he'd done it. Now, after he had stripped them of all their worldly possessions, he'd expel their white asses out of the country. Stubbs glanced hurriedly at East, then quickly turned away from the sight of the man. Too bad, you motherfucka, he thought. There was room only for one winner and he, Maurice J. Stubbs, was it.

SOULFIRE BOOKS

It had all come full circle and by now, everyone in the Court was barely breathing, sitting on the edge of their seats, staring down the throat of the jury foreman. The Judge had finally asked for the verdict.

The rest of the jury looked exhausted and weary, tired from their toil and exertion, but they were insignificant now, inconsequential because the only person that, for the moment, mattered was the foreman who, in his JC Penney suit, was temporarily more important than the President. And whether anyone would ever believe it or not, he was, by and large, right now, the most influential man in the nation.

"Your Honor," the man commenced somberly, "we, the jury, find---."

"*Death to the infidels!*" one of the four, bearded men shouted, jumping nosily to his feet.

The Judge reached for his gavel, but stopped. "Oh no!" he shrieked in terror.

As everyone turned in unison, their faces mirrored the fear the Judge exhibited as they saw that the man's coat was open, exposing a bomb that was strapped around his waist.

"Death to the Great Satan!" The other bearded men sprang to their feet also.

Jamal gasped. Gulliver cursed. East pissed on himself. Stubbs got mad. Peterson prayed. The four men yanked the cords.

KABOOM!!!

The four men exploded, but so did the Courtroom, and everyone in it.

<<<<<<<<<<<<<<<<<
SOULFIRE BOOKS
<<<<<<<<<<<<<<<<<

Not long afterwards.

Herold Pictet, when he found out that the mission was a success, used the time to phone Ibrahim Kunduz to thank him. Then he assembled all the so-called 'Columbus Day' documents before him and abruptly realized he was the wealthiest man in the world. He, alone, owned America because he possessed the deed. It was all his now, lock, stock, and barrel. Everything was his, and there was no one alive who could contest him. Without a doubt, he was in the money.

In Pictet's eyes, all the white man's greed and the black man's cunning had won them nothing. Both had overlooked him, but neither East nor Stubbs had known that winning was second nature to him, and that getting his way had always been the only way he knew when it came to getting what he wanted. But nothing had mattered more than Bill.

That night to celebrate, Herold Pictet dressed in his finest clothes, and went out on the town. He did everything---and more---that he felt befitted a man of his new-found wealth. Then he went home. *Alone.*

The next morning even though he still felt flawed, he was up early. He pondered his personal motto that he never do anything without thinking it over first, and then absently detached himself from what he had decided to do. With grave resignation, but no regret, he flicked on his computer, and without hesitation made some deletions, but when he had finalized the transaction, he wiped his hands symbolically in a cleansing gesture. He had just eliminated all traces of the COLUMBUS DAY DOCUMENTS. It was as they had never existed. As for the ones in his possession, he solemnly gathered them up, dumped them in a ceramic urn, and struck a match to them. The documents burned quickly.

Once they had totally burned, he poured the ashes into a big, brown envelope, and addressed it to the President of the United States. It was a gift from Bill.

Bill had loved America so much that Herold couldn't stand by, and idly watch it destroyed by either one group or the other, so he had to win it. This way he could preserve it, leaving it just as Bill had left it, and for better or worse, Herold Pictet felt he had done the right thing.

Long live America!

SOULFIRE BOOKS

If you liked this novel, then please venture on over to www.soulfirebooks.com to view my other works. Thanks.

www.ingramcontent.com/pod-product-compliance
Lightning Source LLC
Chambersburg PA
CBHW060102260626
47160CB00005B/1766